THE GOVERNOR'S MAN
LEE WILLIAMS

Best Wishes

Lee Williams

THE GOVERNOR'S MAN by Lee Williams

Copyright©2013 by Lee Williams

All rights reserved

No part of this book may be reproduced, stored in, or introduced into a retrieval system, or transmitted in any form, or by any means (electronic, mechanical, photocopying, recording, or otherwise) without the prior written permission of the author.

This is a work of fiction. Names, characters, places, and incidents either are the product of the author's imagination or are used fictitiously. Any resemblance to actual persons, living or dead, events, or locales is entirely coincidental.

Book and cover designed by Ellie Searl, Publishista®

ISBN-10: 0615933394
ISBN-13: 978-0615933399
LCCN: 2013922260

LW Publishing Enterprises
Westmont, IL

BOOKS BY LEE WILLIAMS

IN HIS BLOOD

2009

SINS OF THE FATHER

2011

To my sweet love
Gloria

CHAPTER 1

Kosovo, Bosnia
July 1994
3:00 AM

"LET GO OF ME," MOANED sixteen-year-old Martina as a man pulled her out of the backseat of a rusty Volvo and held her under his arm against his hip. Her black hair knotted into a tangle of ropes contrasted with her pale complexion. Her senses were dulled from the drugs the driver had mixed into a bottle of wine she drank. The stench of his sweaty flesh hit her. She twisted and turned and was dropped into a puddle. She rose onto her hands and knees, mud dripping from her black U-2 T-shirt and white shorts, her sandals lost. She blinked, and the bright glare of an orange neon sign stung her eyes. Tilting her head up, she saw the ink-colored sky. The chatter of men became clear. She looked forward, squinted and saw them bartering for jeans, liquor and guns at wooden huts beside the bar. Martina's eyes cleared and she saw the sign, "The Florida Club."

Someone lifted her by the back of her shorts and T-shirt. Her hands and feet scraped the mixture of asphalt and mud. In front of her were the girls, Elena and Olga, with whom she had shared the back seat of the

Volvo. They had that Eastern European combination of dark hair and chalk-like skin. Elena was chunky, unlike Martina and Olga, who were both slender.

They were herded toward the club by three men with day-old beards who wore wrinkled jeans. One had a New York Yankees' jersey and the other two wore white Armani sweatshirts.

A horde of men turned from the huts and surrounded them, moving in unison toward the club. Some wore military uniforms and carried rifles or wore sidearms. Others were dressed in jeans, dirty T-shirts and mud-caked boots. They closed to within an arm's reach, and she felt their hands groping her. The tangle of their laughter and vulgar words merged into an unintelligible chatter.

Martina was shoved into the club, where the stench of tobacco and beer hit her. A haze of cigarette smoke wafted near the ceiling. To her left were a fake palm tree and the bar. The stools were full of patrons nodding with approval at the three girls. In front of her, blue and red lights pulsated from a jukebox that blasted heavy metal. Across from the bar were waitresses that looked her age, dressed in skimpy tops and short skirts, carried trays of beer steins and shot glasses to four tables filled with men in United Nations' security uniforms and locals in overalls and dusty boots.

A waitress laid her tray on a table. A man in uniform pulled her onto his lap, kissed her neck and forced his hand inside her skirt. His laughter filled the bar. The girl's face was expressionless.

"Luka, open the door," the man behind Martina shouted.

The burly man next to Elena pulled a large key ring out of his pocket with a dozen keys on it. He thumbed through them, picked one out and unlocked a door next to the jukebox. The three girls were herded into a barren room. A light bulb hung from the ceiling. The floor was covered with ten dirty mattresses and a stuffed doll lay on top of a pile of clothing. From the far corner the odor of urine reeked from two buckets. Next to them were four rolls of toilet paper.

Luka kicked the door shut.

Martina shook at the crash.

The brash music and raucous chatter from the bar became distant sounds. Luka pointed to a mattress and nodded at Elena. She shook her head and rubbed her arm where the impressions of Luka's fingers remained. He slapped her and grabbed her blouse at the shoulder, ripping it as he spun her down. Kneeling beside her, he tore it off.

The two men standing behind Olga laughed. One of them put his hand on her shoulder. "Take your clothes off." She pulled her blouse over her head and dropped it to the floor.

Martina turned away, refusing to watch.

"Take your clothes off," the man in the Yankees shirt said.

Martina shook her head. Her wet T-shirt clung to her nipples. She heard the rest of Olga's clothes hit the floor.

"I said, take your clothes off."

Martina glanced over her shoulder and saw Olga pushed to her knees. She turned back and looked into Yankee's soulless eyes.

He pulled a cigarette from a pack of Marlboros and put it in the corner of his mouth. "Be smart like your friends. Take it off." The smoke dangled with each word.

She took a deep breath and felt a hammer beating in her heart. She heard Olga gagging.

"Do it now," he said.

"I would rather die." She spit in his face.

Yankee threw the cigarette down and wiped the back of his hand across his face. His eyes narrowed. "Alexei."

Martina heard Olga stop gagging. Massive arms encased her in a bear hug.

Yankee reached into his pocket and pulled out a black leather case. He slid the zipper around and removed a syringe.

Martina leaned back into Alexei and kicked at Yankee, but she couldn't budge the man behind her. His grip tightened. She gasped for air and felt sweat dripping from his forehead onto her neck.

Yankee moved the syringe in front of her eyes. "I'm a very smart man. I could have Alexei beat the shit out of you. He would like that."

Alexei laughed and she smelled his stale tobacco breath.

"But I don't want to damage my merchandise. Your pretty face will bring me more money if it isn't bruised by my friend's knuckles. A little shot of heroin and you will be very happy to do whatever I ask. Especially next time, because you will be begging for me to give it to you. But you won't get any until you've earned it."

She heard his guttural laugh and felt the needle pierce her skin. It felt like fire bursting through her veins, and then a mellow warmth encompassed her. She grew limp in Alexei's arms and her world turned black.

CHAPTER 2

Chicago
August 1996

SCOTT GARITY'S FACE TURNED CRIMSON. He spun his gold badge across Joe Campos' desk and watched it crash onto his boss's lap.

Campos skidded back in his chair, knocking Richard Volley, Director of the Midwest Federal Drug Task Force, against the credenza behind Campos' desk.

Volley latched onto the credenza trying to regain his balance, cigarette waggling in his mouth. "Now, take it easy. You know we have no choice. There's a bullet in your spine. If something happened on the job and you were paralyzed there'd be all sorts of liability issues."

Scott looked at Volley's potbelly protruding from under his blue-striped tie, where the button of his white shirt had popped off above his belt. "You fucking bureaucrat. For the last three months I've been running three miles a day and lifting four days a week. You're more likely to be found face down on a file folder at your desk than something happening to me."

Scott took a deep breath. He could feel his shirt tighten across his chest. He glanced at Campos, looking for support.

Beads of sweat dripped down his supervisor's brow. Campos glanced at Volley, then back at Scott, and gestured with his hands up and down. "He's just following the manual and—"

Scott shook his head. "Joe, Joe, Joe. I expected something like this from him, but not you."

"Look, you son of a…" Volley folded his lips. "You'll get seventy-five percent disability pay and you can apply for reinstatement in twelve months. But I can't guarantee your reinstatement. You'll have to pass a physical and you'd better show more professionalism and consideration in your demeanor." Volley crossed his arms and rested them on his belly.

Scott brushed his hand through his hair. "I'm going to appeal this to the labor board."

"Don't be a fool, Garity." Volley laughed. "If you lose, you'll never be able to come back, and if Campos and I testify to your vigorous physical activity you'll lose your disability pay. Go ahead if you want to fuck yourself. No skin off my nose."

Scott clenched his teeth.

Volley straightened his tie. "What's your answer?"

Scott swallowed. If he lost his appeal he'd have no income and no pension. He'd have to live off his pension contributions until he found another job. Acid chewed at his stomach. Scott wanted to tell Volley he'd be hearing from his attorney, but he had to think of his son, Billy. "I can apply for reinstatement in twelve months?"

Volley cinched up his slacks, swaying from side to side as he lifted them over his paunch. "That's what the manual says."

Scott nodded and his stomach fired up again. This was almost the only job he knew, but the good memories were fading and the bad ones were haunting him: his lost mentor, crumbling personal life, and the specter of his dark relationship with his father. If he had to slop around for a year it would give him more time to heal. He brushed his hand across his lips, exhaled, and gave Volley the answer Scott was sure he would regret. "Okay."

Volley reached inside his suit coat and whipped out a white envelope. "That's better."

Scott figured the envelope contained the disability agreement. How convenient that Volley had it all prepared. He figured once he signed the form he would never be able to set foot in the task force again. He ran his tongue over his dry lips.

Volley ambled around Campos' desk and stuffed the envelope in Scott's shirt pocket. "My personal advice is to try another line of work while you're off. You might find something more suitable for a man with your…ailment. My uncle's law firm is looking for an investigator. If you think you can work."

"Your uncle?" Scott asked.

Volley cocked his head and raised his eyebrows. "The former governor, James Everson."

Now Scott knew how Volley got the job. *Angels in high places.*

Volley glanced at Campos. "Make sure you get his pistol and any other task force assets—today." He buttoned his suit coat and marched out of the office.

There was a silence in the office as they listened to the click of Volley's heels grow faint.

Campos cleared his throat. "Scott, sometimes it pays to be a go-along guy. Helps you get what you want."

"Prick. If I had one ounce of respect for that fat…." Scott shook his head. "Now we know how he got the job. You think I'm going to work for Everson? I don't kiss anybody's ass."

Campos glanced at the ceiling. "Sit down."

Scott gripped the arms of the chair and eased himself onto the wooden seat.

"I'm glad to hear you're doing well. Why don't you go home and chill? Spend some time with Billy. Enjoy life. I'd love to have a year off to spend with my wife and kids." Campos glanced down. "Sorry, I didn't mean to mention…"

"I'm over her. It died long before she left." Scott shifted in the chair, trying to ease the discomfort he felt from sitting. "Billy's going back to school in a couple of weeks. If I don't have something to do I'll go crazy. I'm sorry, Joe. I know you've got your career and I didn't mean to put you in the middle between me and Volley."

"Don't worry about it." Campos tapped his pen on his desk. "You a need lift home? I can have one of the guys drop you off."

"I've got a doctor's appointment on Michigan Avenue. I'll take a cab and catch the El home." Scott braced his hands on the arms of the chair and eased himself up.

"Before you go, I assume I have all your task force assets." Campos tapped the pen louder.

Scott glanced at the pen. *One bureaucrat was the same as the other.* "Bailey picked up everything the last time he came over to the house." He backed toward the door. "The last thing I had was my badge. You've got that now."

Campos nodded. "Keep in touch. I want you back here next year."

Scott waved and headed to the lobby, walking fast, trying to even his gait so the slight drag in his right leg wouldn't show. He pushed the door open, stepped into the lobby, and watched the door close behind him. It was the first time in almost thirteen years he wasn't a special agent with the task force. He felt like everything he knew about himself was behind that door.

As it clicked shut, pain seared up his spine. He grabbed for the wall and shoved his hand into his pants pocket, searching for a brown plastic vial. He pulled it out and slid down the wall to the floor. He squeezed his eyes together as the pain shot up the back of his neck. He felt like his head was splitting. He twisted the white top. It spun off as his fingers cramped. The vial fell to the floor and pills spilled across the dusty tile. Scott grabbed a handful of Vicodin and shoved them into his mouth, hoping no one would enter the lobby.

Chapter 3

Chicago, Early September 1996
Wednesday, 12:45 AM

Victor Marchese leaned back in his chair, exhaled, pulled in his gut and unbuttoned the slacks of his designer suit. It seemed like every few months he had to have his tailor let out his slacks again. He kicked his feet on top of his mahogany desk and dragged a file across his manicured fingernails. He'd had to hang around his office late to get the package, but it was worth it. "If I know one thing for sure, in Chicago it's good to be a Democrat."

He looked with pride at his title, Deputy Commissioner, printed in black on the frosted glass set in the top half of his door. He had worked hard for thirty years and now he was reaping the benefits. He patted his soft tummy, swung his feet down and blew the dried skin off his fingernails.

"Time to combine pleasure and business." He drained the glass of eighteen-year-old Macallan Scotch he had poured while waiting for the package and glanced out the window at the office building lights brightening the Loop late into the night. Out of curiosity he lifted the envelope off his desk blotter and peeled it open. *He'll never know.* He dragged his thumb through an inch of hundred-dollar bills. "Ben Franklin, one of my favorite Founding Fathers. One more delivery for the Gov, one more blow job for me." He pushed himself away from his desk and lumbered to the garage.

Marchese got into his black Cadillac, pulled out of the underground parking lot and headed south on LaSalle. The streets were empty except for a work van parked opposite the parking garage's exit ramp.

FBI agent Ed Francis keyed his microphone. "All units be advised he's six on financial."

The four cars on the surveillance responded, "Ten-four."

"Over to Wells and six again. Nine on the president," Baxter said over the radio.

The agents followed Marchese as he drove west on the Eisenhower Expressway, exited north on Mannheim Road and drove for several miles.

"He's pulling into the parking lot of the Pole Club, a strip joint," Agent Richmond said. "These joints have a two a.m. liquor license on weekdays so he's only got half an hour before closing time. Baxter, you're the rookie and you look less like an agent than us old timers. Follow him into the club and see what he's up to."

"You think there's a cover charge? Could I get reimbursed?"

"You're getting paid for looking at naked women. What more do you want?"

Marchese parked near the club's sign, a silhouette of a shapely woman with one leg wrapped around a pole. He walked to the main entrance where two off-duty cops handled security. They greeted him and waved him through without the pat-down reserved for gangbangers or unfamiliar clients that came to the club.

Baxter followed. He wore black horn-rimmed glasses, khaki slacks, a blue polo shirt and white tennis shoes. His dark hair was neatly cut and parted on the side. The cops took his five-dollar cover and patted him down. *Lucky I left my hardware in the car*, he thought.

He entered the club. The pounding beat of the music blasted against his chest and he saw three women wearing nothing but garters gyrating against brass poles mounted on the V-shaped bar. Lights flashed from the ceiling onto their bodies, changing from red to green and then blue. Thin lines of green laser light swept across the girls. Men were standing three deep behind the bar stools, leaning over the seated patrons and stuffing cash into the girls' garters.

Baxter stopped at the top of the V. A blonde leaned her back against the pole and slid down onto her haunches. She pointed an index finger at him and lowered it between her legs, smiled and rotated her tongue around her lips.

He took a step back, felt his groin hardening and exhaled. *Never saw anything like that in Iowa.*

A waitress stepped up to him. She wore pasties and a G-string. "Two-drink minimum, honey."

He shook his head and remembered why he was there.

"Sorry, honey. Two-drink minimum means two drinks. What'll you have?"

"Ah, Coke." He took his eyes off the pasties and scanned the room for Marchese.

"It's sixteen bucks for Coke or booze."

"I don't drink."

"Gimme your money and I'll get you your pop."

Baxter pulled his wallet out of his back pocket and fingered through the bills, giving her six singles and a ten.

"You know it's legal in this state to tip your service personnel, especially in a place like this. I mean, with all the T & A in your face."

He opened his wallet again and put a single on her tray.

"Oh God, another high roller. It's my lucky night." She turned and strutted away.

Baxter's gaze followed the thin line of cloth that separated her butt cheeks. He dragged the back of his forearm across his forehead, wiping off perspiration. He glanced around the bar and saw Marchese talking to a man who looked like an offensive tackle for the Bears. Veined biceps jutted out of the sleeves of his black t-shirt. The bouncer, Baxter assumed, and moved closer to listen in.

"Where's Ivanov?" Marchese asked.

"He left early. Wife sick," Luka said. His forehead bulged over his eyes like a Cro-Magnon man.

"Call him. Tell him I've got business for him."

"He went home, to Lake Forest. He no come back tonight. Too far."

"You call him and tell him to get his ass here. I've come for the governor." Marchese lowered his head. He knew he'd said too much.

Luka smiled. "I do business with you and tell Mr. Ivanov tomorrow."

"You call him now and let me talk to him. Then we'll see."

"I call. You wait here, yes?"

"You call him now and I'll wait inside the VIP room. No, wait. First you bring Marti to me. Then you call him and come back and tell me what he wants to do. Come back in twenty-five minutes." Marchese's heart raced in anticipation. He watched Luka walk past the point of the bar and down the other side, where he entered the door leading to the office.

Marchese stepped into the VIP room and locked the door. He helped himself to the wine refrigerator, removed a bottle of Cristal and popped the cork. He lifted two champagne glasses off the shelf above the refrigerator, filled them and placed one on a black coffee table in front of the matching leather couch. He took two purple pills out of his pants pocket and downed them with the champagne. He refilled his glass, sat down and loosened his belt.

A few minutes later the curtain across from him stirred. "Hello, Victor," she whispered. "It's Marti. Are you ready?"

"Come here. I've been waiting."

She poked her face through the curtain. Her high cheekbones were sprinkled with glitter that swept into platinum hair. Then a long leg split the curtain, a serpent's-tail tattoo twisting up and around from the ankle over and behind her thigh. On her foot was a golden shoe with a spiked heel. "Do you want me?"

Marchese pulled down his zipper, "Yes. Yes, Marti. Victor wants you."

"What do you have for me?" She touched the tip of her nose with her diamond-studded tongue.

He leaned over the coffee table, pulled a glass vial out of his pocket and removed the lid. "I have this for you." He poured three lines of white powder onto a small mirror on the tabletop.

"That's all?" She pulled her leg back behind the curtain.

"No, no, I have more." He laid two one-hundred dollar bills next to the powder.

Marti pulled the curtain open and stepped out. Her firm young naked body glistened in the black light. She did a pirouette, bowing in front of him. The nipples on her enhanced breasts pointed to the ceiling. She spun around, revealing the serpent's head tattooed across her back, its red eyes and split black tongue reaching to her shoulder.

Marchese groaned, picked up his glass of Cristal and drained it.

She stepped around the table, grabbed one of the Franklins, rolled it into a short straw and straddled him. "You so good to me. You take first toot."

He leaned forward, placed his index finger against one nostril and the curled bill in the other, and snorted. He felt her hand slip into his pants. His heart quickened and his face warmed. "Don't stop. Let me have another line."

She held the mirror up to his nose and kept pumping him.

He raised the bill to his face, snorted and fell onto the mirror. It crashed to the floor. Cocaine floated through the air and onto Marti.

"You silly goof. See what you did?" She pushed him against the back of the sofa. "You got coke all over you." She gently brushed the powder off his cheek. "Victor. Victor?" Her eyes narrowed. "Victor!"

His body lay still.

"Victor, stop it. This isn't funny." Marti grabbed the lapels of his suit coat and shook him. There was no response. She shook him harder and an envelope fell out of his pocket. She paid it no heed, breathing fast as memories of death and destruction from Bosnia flashed through her mind. This was the first time she had seen a dead man since then. *What would Ivanov do to her for killing a client?* She sat back on her haunches.

A voice came from behind the locked door. "Mr. Marchese, it's Luka." She heard the door banging against its frame as he tried to open it. "Mr. Marchese," he shouted.

"We're not done, Luka." she shouted back. "Come back in ten minutes."

"Mr. Ivanov will be here in a few minutes. He didn't go home. His wife felt better."

"Go, Luka, not now." She got off Marchese, heart pounding.

"Okay. I will have Mr. Ivanov come get him when he arrives, yes?"

"Go, Luka."

She heard his footsteps moving off. The envelope from Victor's pocket caught her eye. She picked it up, peeled it open and eyed the stash of greenbacks inside. "Holy shit." She searched his other pockets and found his key chain, wallet, a spiral notebook the size of a credit card and $400 in cash. She put the keychain back, stashed everything in the envelope and rushed toward the curtain. She heard Luka's voice outside as she reached it: "He's with Marti, Mr. Ivanov."

The door rattled in its frame. "Open the door, Marti," Ivanov said.

She hesitated, then did as he ordered, hiding the envelope behind her thigh. "Mr. Ivanov, something's wrong with Mr. Marchese," she said. "He…"

Ivanov rushed past her into the VIP room. He knelt and pressed his fingers against Marchese's neck. "Luka, call 911. I don't feel a pulse. Hurry, hurry." He glanced up at Marti. "Martina, go tell Yuri to come in here and clean this coke up before the paramedics get here."

Marti rushed through the curtain and snatched up the robe she'd dropped to the floor. She hid the envelope under the robe, cinched the belt tight and headed to the dressing room. Two dancers, Nadia and Tanya, sat in similar robes in front of dressing mirrors, taking off their makeup. Marti's abrupt entrance made them both look up.

Marti swallowed hard. "Nadia, please tell Yuri to go the VIP room. I think Victor is dead and I'm going to be sick."

Shock spread over both their faces. Tanya nudged Nadia. "Go, I'll help Marti."

Nadia rushed out.

Tanya turned to Marti. "What happened, honey?"

"Don't have time to tell you now. I'm getting out," Marti whispered. "I'm not going back to the apartment with the rest of you."

The blaring music from the club stopped, and Marti could hear sirens from the approaching ambulance. A man's voice came over the sound system: "Due to an emergency, the club is closing. Please exit in an orderly fashion."

"I have to go now." Marti dropped her robe, stepped into panties and blue jeans, stuck the envelope in her back pocket, pulled a T-shirt and a hooded black sweatshirt over her head and slipped on a pair of boots. "The van will be here any minute to take the girls to the apartment."

Tanya turned away from the mirror and stood. "You won't get away. They'll get you and then Marko will beat you within an inch of your life. What will you do for money? You think you can trick on your own without Ivanov finding you?" Her eyes welled.

Marti put her arms around Tanya and kissed her. "I won't leave you. I love you."

"What will you do for dope?"

Marti's lips pursed. "I'll send for you when I'm clean. Goodbye, Tanya."

Drazen Ivanov stood over Marchese's body, *He only comes here when he thinks the Governor's money entitles him to a free blow job.* He slipped his hand into the man's inside suit coat pockets, searching for the usual envelope full of cash. "Nothing." His eyes narrowed and he patted down Marchese's pants pockets. Car keys, but no money. "Luka, roll this pig over and check his back pockets." He stepped to the side and watched Luka strain as he rolled the fat man over.

"No wonder you had a heart attack, you fat slob," Luka said as he slipped his fingers into Marchese's rear pockets. "No wallet. No loose cash."

"Fuck, that bitch must have taken his wallet." Ivanov looked up at the ceiling, "Goddamn it."

Yuri opened the door, holding a bucket and a hand-held vacuum cleaner. "Nadia tell me you want me to clean up?"

"Clean the powder off him right now," Ivanov said. "Do it fast. Paramedics are on the way."

"Yes, sir."

"Luka, come with me." They stepped through the curtain into the hallway leading to the dressing room. "I'm going to the lounge area to make sure customers leave before the paramedics and cops get here. You go to the dressing room and get Marti. That fucking bitch stole the wallet off a dead man." He shook his head. "She uses any of his credit cards, it will draw attention to us. Get Marchese's stuff back."

"Then I slap her around, yes?"

"First get her and the girls out of here, fast. When you get them to the apartment, teach her a lesson. It will be good for the other girls to see."

Chapter 4

Wednesday, 2:00 AM

MARTI CREPT OUT OF THE dressing room into the dimly lit hallway that led to the back door. She knew this was the time to escape. Between the paramedics rushing in to take Marchese's body, cops roaming around the club and Ivanov's people ushering the customers out, everyone's attention would be in the front of the club.

She stopped at the rear door and remembered what Ivanov's son, Marko, told her in Bosnia two years ago. *"We will get you to the West. You work off your fee and you will be free before you know it."*

She knew now it was all a lie. She wouldn't be free until they didn't need her any more. What they charged her for rent, food and medical bills was more than the cash she gave them every night. Of course, the heroin was free, because it kept her a prisoner until they didn't need her. When the whoring and the dope aged her beyond her years she would be replaced by another naïve teenager. *God knows what will happen to me then.*

Marti exhaled and closed her eyes. Her hands trembled as she pushed against the release bar, opening the door a crack. She peered through the opening. There were five cars parked in the back lot, Ivanov's shiny new Lexus and other vehicles belonging to employees. But no one was in the lot. She stepped onto the asphalt and heard the door click shut behind her. She bit her lip and realized the odds were against her. She had been smuggled into the country and had no papers. She clutched the envelope in her back pocket. *This is my only hope.*

She took another step and the security light with the motion detector flooded the parking lot. She froze. Beams from the headlights of the van came around the corner. She dove behind the dumpster next to the door. The envelope fell out and landed an arm's length away. Her hope for the future lay on the grimy asphalt. The smell of rancid food invaded her senses as she inhaled.

The van stopped three feet away. Ivan, the driver, stepped out. His pale, thin arms clashed with his black T-shirt and jeans. His hair was cropped close to his skull. He rushed around the front of the van toward the rear entrance, probably hoping to catch the girls in the dressing room naked. He stopped at the door. The envelope lay three inches behind his heel. Ivan took a drag on his cigarette and flicked it to the pavement, crushing it with the toe of his shoe. He pulled the door open and entered.

Marti knew he would linger in the dressing room for at least fifteen minutes. She grabbed the envelope and ran as fast as she could to the alley adjoining the parking lot and headed north. Her lungs burned and sweat rolled down her face.

She stopped at a dumpster behind a restaurant and opened the envelope. She had overheard Marko talking about stealing credit cards, so she pulled out anything that looked like a credit card from Marchese's wallet, threw the wallet and the rest of the contents into the dumpster.

In another five minutes they would be looking for her. She went to the rear corner of the restaurant and saw three cabs lined up in front. She pursed her lips and ran to the first cab. The van with the dancers passed the restaurant, heading north. Behind it was Marko driving a black Mercedes. A customer opened the rear passenger door of the cab for his date and Marti dived into the rear seat.

"What's happening, my lady?" the driver said. He wore a red, green and yellow dread cap, and cornrows of hair fell to his shoulders

"Go that way." She pointed south, in the opposite direction of Marko and the van. She peered through the rear window and saw the taillights of the Mercedes getting smaller. "Go, go."

Baxter watched the paramedics rush into the club and head toward the VIP room as the bouncers herded him out of the club with the rest of the customers. He ran to senior agent William Richmond's car and jumped into the passenger seat.

"What the hell happened?" Richmond asked.

"I don't know. Marchese went into the VIP room. Some burly guy followed him in and left a few minutes later. Fifteen, twenty minutes after that, the burly guy comes back with an older fellow. They went into the VIP room. A little while later they announced over the PA system that the club was closing for the night. Then the paramedics came in and rushed toward the VIP room."

"What did those two guys look like—the burly guy and the one with him?" Richmond asked.

"The burly guy was in his late twenties, maybe early thirties, just under six feet, had to weigh at least two hundred and thirty pounds. Looked like a weightlifter. Oh yeah, shaved head and dressed in black."

"And the older guy?"

"Sixties, short black hair with lots of gray. Probably five feet nine, one hundred sixty pounds. He was the boss. He was telling the big guy what to do, pointing him in one direction and then another."

Richmond nodded. "Good job, Baxter. Write up your three-oh-two tonight and tomorrow you contact the paramedics and get their report."

Marko followed the van north for two miles, then east into a neighborhood full of Section 8 apartment buildings. The van rocked down a gravel alley and parked behind a six-flat next to a car sitting on milk crates. Marko's cell phone rang. He saw his father's number. "Yes?"

"You find Marti?"

"No, she's not in the van."

"Shit. Marchese told Luka he had a package for me but I find nothing and his wallet's missing. Bitch must have taken it. She can't have gone too far. I got the bouncers checking the streets. We can't let her get away. Talk to the girls. One of them must know the bitch's plan."

"Okay, Papa." Marko turned off his cell and parked his Mercedes behind an apartment building.

He watched Ivan hustle the six girls from the van to the rear door of the next building. The scrawny man pulled a long chain from his pants pocket, the other end clipped to his belt. At the end of the chain was a ring with two dozen keys that could gain access to the various apartment buildings and strip-mall shopping centers that Ivanov owned under a variety of front corporations. Ivan fumbled through the keys while keeping an eye on the girls.

Marko thought, *I know that little pimp is hoping one of the girls will be nice to him. But there is no time for that now—not with a dead bagman and missing cash.*

Ivan found the key for the deadbolt and unlocked the door. The girls knew the routine, marching up three flights of stairs to the top floor. There were two apartments on that floor, both used by Ivanov's operation. One stored stolen merchandise and items purchased with credit card numbers skimmed by electronic readers planted in the pumps at gas stations the Russian owned. The other apartment, a two-bedroom unit with burglar bars on the windows, was for the girls.

Upstairs, Ivan went through the same procedure, unlocking the deadbolt for the apartment. The girls strolled in and draped themselves on the two worn sofas in the living room that together formed an L shape. Ivan handed out cigarettes or joints, depending on their choice.

He pulled a gold Dunhill lighter from his jeans. "See this, a gift from the boss. I call him by his first name, Drazen. He likes me. You would be wise to like me, too. I can help you with any wish you may have." He went from girl to girl, lighting their smokes with one hand and stroking their legs with the other. He nodded to himself, jammed an Auktyon CD into the player and gyrated his hips in front of the girls. "My favorite rock band from home. You like?"

The girls giggled. Ivan stopped dancing, grabbed a bottle and a shot glass from a makeshift bar across from the sofas. "A shot of vodka, yes?"

Veronika, a slender blonde, spoke up. "I don't feel like giving another blow job, little man." She slouched against the back of the sofa, her long legs splayed in tight-fitting jeans.

"I not like that, just trying to help you unwind after a hard night's work." His tongue circled his lips.

The door crashed against the wall. Ivan dropped the bottle and the girls huddled together on the sofas.

"Where the fuck is Marti?" Marko shouted from the doorway. His chest was thick and the vein in his throat bulged. He took a step into the room and slammed the door shut. "I hear nothing." His eyes raked across each girl's face.

Tanya lowered her head and stared at her black boots. Her red hair fell around her face.

Marko lowered his voice. "If any of you know where she is, my father will be very appreciative."

Veronika pointed at Tanya. "Ask Lover Girl. I'm sure they have a secret rendezvous arranged."

Tanya pursed her lips and shook her head.

Nataliya jumped to her feet and stabbed a finger at Tanya. "The lesbian sisters keep to their selves. They make us stay in one room so they can eat pussy. Fuck them, they get us all in trouble."

Marko rolled up the sleeves of his black shirt, stomped to the couch, and extended his meaty hand. He locked it around Tanya's throat and yanked her up, then spun around and jammed her against the wall. "Where is she?"

"I know nothing." Gasping for air, she could barely squeeze the words out of her mouth.

"Liar," Marko said, spit flying onto Tanya's face. He banged her head against the wall. "Tell me."

She coughed as his grip tightened.

"Tell me now or else." Marko whipped a switchblade out of his pants pocket. The blade snapped out and he slit the skin under her right eye. "Not much demand for a one-eyed whore."

Tanya cried out. Blood dripped down her cheek. "She said she was going to get clean. That Victor was dead. That's all I know. Then she went out the back door just before Ivan came."

Marko looked over his shoulder. "Ivan, put the rest of the girls in their room and get their fixes ready."

The girls hustled into one of the bedrooms, sticking together like a flock of frightened birds. Ivan closed the bedroom door, locking them inside, then went to the refrigerator and removed a handful of tinfoil packets. He took the packets to the stove and turned on the flame.

Marko lowered the blade. "My father would not be happy with me if I took your eye. Ivan, don't make Tanya's fix tonight. We'll see what else she has to tell us in the morning when she's begging for smack." He loosened his fingers and Tanya slid down the wall into a heap.

She grazed her finger across the cut below her eye, glanced at the blood on it and looked up at him. "The only other thing I know is, she said that she will come back for me when she is clean…and that…and that she loves me. I will let you know when she gets in touch with me." She extended her forearm in Marko's direction. "I don't want to be sick."

Marko slapped it away. "I will see what you know when I come back in ten hours."

Chapter 5

Wednesday, 2:15 AM

The cabby steered away from the curb. "You shouldn't be in such a hurry. It'll stress you out."

Marti opened the envelope, left the cash and the little notebook in it, and spread the cards across the back seat. Two credit cards and four ATM cards.

They stopped at a red light. Marti raised her head and saw the Pole Club. The ambulance was parked in front along with two squad cars. Their lights flashed across the parking lot as customers entered their cars and drove away. She threw herself down on the seat.

"Some poor soul must have had a heart attack watching the girlies," the driver said.

Marti raised herself just high enough to peer out the window at the parking lot. She recognized two of the bouncers, Boris and Zoran, standing at the front entrance. Paramedics were rolling the gurney with Marchese's body into the ambulance. She closed her eyes and lowered herself beneath the protection of the door. Her chest expanded and contracted with each rapid breath.

"You all right, lady?"

She said nothing, waiting to gather her senses. The stoplight turned green and the cabbie pulled away. She clung to the seat and waited.

"Miss, you really stressed out. You need something to smoke?"

Marti sat up. "Yes." Then she thought what if a cop pulled them over and found the cash and credit cards on her. "No, no." She shuffled the credit and ATM cards. She remembered customers at the club slipping the cards into the machine and getting cash back to slip in her garters. Holding the cards like a poker hand, she read the first one out loud: "First National Bank."

"There's one right by the expressway. You need to get some cash?"

She nodded. "I do, yes."

Ten minutes later the cab pulled next to an ATM machine in one of the bank's drive-thru aisles.

Marti opened the rear door and jumped out, pulled her hood low over her face and stepped in front of the machine. She slipped the card into it. On the screen, the keypad popped up with instructions to enter her PIN number. "Shit." Her chin dropped to her chest. She exhaled, hit the cancel button and retrieved the card. She turned toward the cab, opened the door, sat down and slammed it shut.

"What's wrong?" the cabbie said.

"Nothing."

"I bet you forgot your pin number."

"Pin number?" She'd seen the words on the screen, but didn't understand the term.

"Yeah, you know, secret code, whatever they call it." He waved his hand. "Didn't you write it down?"

Write it down. Marti thought. She pulled the envelope out of her back pocket again, opened it and slipped out the spiral notebook. She flipped through the pages, and on page three found a list of four banks with four-digit numbers next to each bank's name. She opened the door, stepped over to the ATM machine and inserted the card, then glanced at the notebook and punched in the numbers. The screen listed several withdrawal options. She pushed the button for $500. Twenty-five $20 bills dropped into the tray. She went through the same process twice more before the screen flashed the message, "No further transactions allowed." She got back into the cab and looked at the driver's ID tag. "Thank you, Jamal," she said as she pushed five twenties through the divider separating the front seat from the back.

By four a.m. they had gone to three banks that matched the remaining ATM cards Marti had taken from Marchese, where she withdrew another $1,500 from each bank and filled the envelope with the cash.

A craving stirred in her mind. It had been over twenty-four hours since her last taste of heroin. *I have the money for rehab, I need one last spike to get me through until I can check in somewhere.* Sweat trickled from her armpits down her torso. "Jamal, can you stop somewhere? I need to use a bathroom."

"Yes, Miss. I need gas. I pull into the first station we come to."

"Please hurry." She dragged the sleeve of her sweatshirt across her nose.

A few minutes later, he pulled into a gas station. She saw the attendant inside staring at her as she jumped out of the back seat and ran toward the bathroom door on the side of the building. She cranked the doorknob, but it didn't turn.

Someone knocked on the plate glass window nearby. The sound caught Marti's attention. She ran around the corner of the station, tightening her muscles as she felt diarrhea dripping down her leg. She saw the clerk holding a long wooden dowel with a steel ring on the end that held the key. She rushed inside, grabbed the key without saying a word to him and headed back out to the bathroom. She entered and flicked on the light. The floor was filthy, the mirror cracked and the water in the toilet bowl rust-colored. She pulled down her pants and panties, and sat as her insides rushed out of her. She could feel her muscles aching as she wiped the insides of her panties clean with toilet paper. *One more time. Then I start a new day tomorrow. A new life.*

She rejoined Jamal in the cab. "I need to score some smack. You know a place?"

He started the cab and pulled onto the street. "Got to go down to the expressway. Get to the West Side to K-town."

She slipped another $100 out of the envelope, slid it into the tray and saw Jamal grab it. She stashed $60 in her front jeans pocket, another $100 in her back pocket and the rest in the envelope, which she tucked down the front of her jeans.

Jamal sped down the expressway. He headed east, exiting at Laramie Avenue to Madison. Red and green lights flashed across the pavement from the neon signs of Daddy Nail's Place and The Player's Club. The last of the players, wearing designer clothes, strutted toward their shiny Cadillacs with their ladies sashaying behind them dressed in spandex and gold jewelry.

Jamal turned north on Kildare into a different world.

Most of the light bulbs in the lampposts were shot out. Courtyard buildings had boarded-up windows, their bricks tinged black from fires or covered with burglar bars. Five young black men stood near the corner. Jamal pulled up to the curb.

"Hey, nigger, what's goin' on," a teenage boy said. He wore a Bulls T-shirt, baggy shorts hanging from his hips, and Jordan basketball shoes.

Jamal palmed him a twenty. "My lady friend needs to shoot up. She got the cash. What's good tonight?"

"Go to the 206 building. It's the one with the little lamppost in front. Apartment 2B. Got everything she need. She get hassled, tell the man Patchie sent her."

Jamal pulled away as Patchie pulled out a cell phone and called ahead.

The brakes squealed as he double-parked in front of 206. "Hey, lady, you here. Go to this building right here, Apartment 2B." He pointed at the lamppost." They give you a problem, tell 'em Patchie sent you."

Marti rubbed her eyes and stared out the window. Her legs were cramping. "Where are we?"

"K-town, on the West Side like I told you."

"My legs are hurting."

Jamal shut the engine off, got out of the cab and opened the rear door. He pulled her out of the back seat and guided her to the front entrance. The wooden door had six bullets holes scattered across it. He pushed it open, put his arm under hers and helped her up the steps. With each footfall, the steps creaked. A dim light from a cracked wall sconce cast their shadows down the stairs. At the second floor he walked her to 2B. The number was scrawled on the door with a black marker. He knocked.

A voice came through the door. "What the fuck you want?"

"Patchie sent us."

A deadbolt clicked and the door opened. A thin black man stood there, holding a revolver in his right hand. His front tooth was missing, the others yellow. "What's her problem?"

"She a little sick. Needs some smack."

"She smells bad, fuckin' junkies."

"Take her, she got money. Nothin' else matter." Jamal handed Marti over to the man. He placed his arm where Jamal's had been, brought her inside a step, kicked the door closed and locked the deadbolt.

He walked her into what was once a living room. She saw the remnants of a built-in buffet with matching wood trim from what looked like decades ago, but no furniture. Plastic garbage bags covered the windows. Junkies lay on dingy mattresses spread across the floor. Several had needles sticking out of their arms as their minds floated into some other reality. The man took Marti to an empty mattress, bent on one knee and laid her down. He shook her shoulder. "You got money?"

She pulled the $60 out of her pocket and handed it to him.

He got up and went into the kitchen. Five minutes later he returned with a syringe, a thin rubber tube and four tinfoil packets. He dropped the packets on her lap, wrapped the tube around her right bicep and flicked her blood vessel with his index finger. Then he held the syringe up and pushed the plunger until a few drops bled down the needle. He stuck it into Marti's blood vessel and pushed the plunger all the way. She groaned and her eyelids gently closed. Her mouth opened as if she was having an orgasm. He removed the tube from her bicep and left the syringe in her arm. "Gave ya four dime bags and a hypo. I'm a honest business man." He pushed himself up and returned to the kitchen where an old episode of *Gunsmoke* was on the TV.

CHAPTER 6

Wednesday, 7:30 AM

SCOTT SWUNG HIS LEGS OVER the side of the bed. He grabbed a brown plastic bottle next to his wallet on the night stand and shook it. Three pills rattled inside. He swiped his hand across his face and read the fine print on the bottle: *No refills*. He slammed the bottle down, picked up his wallet and grabbed the cash out of it. *Three hundred bucks.*

His eyes drifted to the alarm clock. "Holy shit. Billy, get up, you're going to be late for school." There was no response. He grabbed his jeans off the floor, pulled them on, yanked on his T-shirt from the foot of the bed and stepped into his jogging shoes, stumbling into the hallway as he yelled at Billy's bedroom door. "Get up. You're going to be late. I'll drive you."

"Don't sweat it." Billy's voice came from the kitchen downstairs.

"Don't be a wise ass. I don't want you late for school."

"Dad, I got breakfast made for you and me and I made my lunch, too. Come down and eat and then you can drive me."

"Oh. Okay. I'll be right down." Scott went into the bathroom and looked in the mirror. "I look like shit." He had lost weight and could see it in his bony cheeks. He turned on the water, splashed his face, combed his hair with his fingers and plodded downstairs.

"I got Wheaties with a sliced banana and a glass of OJ for you," Billy said, shoving a spoonful of cereal into his mouth.

"Don't have the time. Got to get you to school and I've got errands to run." Scott grabbed the orange juice and downed it.

"You said breakfast is the most important meal. That—"

"Hurry up. We have to leave in two minutes or you'll be late." He slammed the glass down on the kitchen table. His hand trembled. "I'll be in the car."

"Dad, are you okay?"

"Yeah. Hurry, Billy. I'm going to the car. You're not there in two minutes, I'm gonna have to go without you."

Billy lowered his head, "I made breakfast for you so we could eat together."

"In the car, now." He grabbed Billy's hand and pulled him off the chair.

"Dad, my lunch."

"Where the hell is it?" Scott closed his eyes and pursed his lips. He knew the pills were getting the best of him.

"In the fridge."

Scott let go of Billy's hand, opened the refrigerator, and pulled out the paper bag and a can of Pepsi. "Let's go, now."

Scott pulled his '89 Cutlass out of the garage and headed to St. Mary's on the north side of Oak Park. "There's a new basketball coach this year, Father Hanley," Billy said.

Scott was silent, his mind focused on the cash in his wallet that was all that was left from his disability check, the $250 it was going to cost him to satisfy his need for the day and how he was going to pay his mortgage. Billy's conversation was white noise.

"Dad, what do you think about us having a new coach?"

Scott pulled up to the school. "It's almost seven forty-five. Isn't that when your first class starts? You better go."

Billy jumped out of the car without a word. His head down, feet dragging, he headed to the school's front door.

Scott turned south toward Lake Street. He drove through Oak Park, past its trendy restaurants and coffee shops to Austin Boulevard, and then headed south to Madison, entering Chicago's West Side. He popped the lid on the Pepsi, gulped a slug down and put the can between his legs.

The storefronts became dry cleaners, packaged goods stores, and bars. Even at this time of the morning, he saw customers waiting for the barred security doors to open and men standing on corners taking drinks out of brown paper bags. As he drove past Cicero Avenue, the sidewalks grew more crowded with people who looked like they had no place to go. He got to K town and knew it didn't matter too much which street he headed up. He turned north on Kostner and three blocks later pulled to the curb. A teenage boy stood on the corner, a wad of cash in one hand.

The boy stepped up to Scott. "Hey, man, you want some toot?"

"No, pills. You got any Vicodin or Oxy?"

"Shit, man, I don't handle that stuff. See the nigger on the next corner. He do that." He stepped back, jerked his head toward the rear of Scott's car and mumbled. "Five-oh, five-oh."

Scott's eyes flashed to the rearview mirror. Pulling up behind him was a squad car. His fingers tightened on the steering wheel. *Got nothing on me. Don't worry.* Beads of sweat dripped down the back of his neck and saturated his T-shirt.

The doors on the squad car opened and slammed shut.

Scott's gaze danced from one side-view mirror to the other—men in blue uniforms marching toward his car on both sides. The cop approaching his door locked his fingers around his pistol grips.

"License and registration," the cop said.

Scott glanced at the officer's name plate. "Yes, sir, Officer Marotti." He pulled out his wallet, slipped out his license, got his registration out of the glove compartment and handed them to the cop.

"You live in Oak Park. What are you doin' here, Mr. Garity?"

Scott folded his lips, looked at the officer and then glanced down. "My kid. I think he might be buying drugs out here. He's been hanging out with some older kids and a bunch of them cut school today. I'm driving around to see if I can find him and warning these pushers not to sell to him."

"So if I frisk you, I won't find anything?"

"Nope, not me. Never touch that stuff."

"What's your kid's name?"

"Billy. He's twelve, but I'm afraid these older kids are gonna get him in trouble."

"Mr. Garity, go home. You drive around here, only something bad will happen. We'll keep our eyes peeled for your boy. Give me your telephone number and your son's description." Marotti handed the license and registration back.

"Like I said, he's twelve, about five-two, a hundred twenty-five pounds, light brown hair, fair complexion." Scott gave the cop his phone number. "Thanks, Officer." He nodded at Marotti, returned his license to his wallet, the registration to the glove box, and pulled away from the curb.

"Bet that kid is a snitch," Scott mumbled. He drove to the next corner, turned east and parked in front of an old jeep on milk crates. He focused on his side-view mirror, waiting for the cops to go past him so he could find the boy with the pills. The reflections of three cars flashed by in the mirror, each one looking like a prospective customer of the boy he wanted to see. A few minutes later he saw the squad car head north past the street he was parked on.

Scott thumped his fingers on the steering wheel, giving the cops time to get out of the neighborhood. "Just my luck the kid will run out by the time I get to him." He pulled away from the curb, headed to the next corner, turned south and then headed west, parking short of Kostner. *Wait to see if the cops circle around.*

Ten minutes later, Scott headed north on Kostner. *Marotti hit this block once, odds are he's in a different sector now.* He drove past the kid he'd stopped at the first time and two blocks further pulled to the curb. A young black boy loitered there, heavy-set, jeans hanging from his hips exposing black boxer shorts. Tucked into his shorts was a green Celtics jersey.

"Looking for Vicodin," Scott said.

"Gimme two-fifty. My partner's kitty corner." He nodded at another boy in a Celtics jersey. "He give you whats you want."

Scott slipped him the rolled-up bills. "You better not be scamming me."

"I be straight up, man."

Scott yanked the steering wheel and turned a semicircle to the opposite corner. The boy handed him a potato chip bag. Scott opened it and glanced in. He saw what he needed, headed back to Madison Street and westbound. *Need to take the edge off.*

He slipped his hand into the potato chip bag, grabbed three pills, tossed them in his mouth and downed them with the Pepsi. A shrieking siren blasted through him. He spilled the soda into his lap and glanced in the rearview mirror. He saw a flashing blue light. *Fuck, I'm busted.* He pulled to the curb, lowered his head and waited for the cop.

"Mr. Garity."

Scott glanced up. "Officer Marotti, could you give me some professional courtesy? It's a minor problem."

"What?" Marotti's forehead furrowed. "I just wanted to tell you we found your son."

Scott stashed the potato chip bag under the seat and followed the squad car to the police station in the Harrison District. It was the newest building in the area but poverty and desperation were still winning the war. The squad parked behind the building and Scott parked on the street.

Scott entered through the front door.

Marotti was standing with one hand on Billy's shoulder in front of the bulletproof glass that protected the desk sergeant. "Here's your dad,

Billy. You two go home, have a nice talk, and hopefully we'll never run into each other again."

Billy bit his lip and hung his head.

"Thanks, Officer," Scott said. "I appreciate you watching out for my boy."

"I called your cell and left a message on your voicemail. You must have had your phone turned off."

Scott pulled his phone off his belt and looked at the black display. He exhaled. "Yeah, guess I did. Don't know what was on my mind. Thanks again. Let's go home, Billy."

They walked out the door to the Olds and got in. There was no conversation for ten minutes, while Scott's face grew redder. "I dropped you off at school," he said finally. "What the hell were you doing on the West Side? You could have been killed."

Billy folded his arms across his chest. "The cop told me you were out there looking for me. How did you know I was there?"

"You don't ask the questions. I'm the father. I ask the questions. Why were you there?"

Tears ran down Billy's face. He turned toward the passenger window.

Scott slammed the steering wheel with his fist. "Billy, damn it, why were you there?"

"Don't you think I know something is wrong with you, Dad? Are you sick? The only times you talk to me, you yell. You don't care what I'm doing. I played the message on the answering machine. The man from the bank said you hadn't paid the mortgage. Are they gonna take our house?"

Scott swallowed and curled his lips. "No, I'm just a few weeks late. They won't take the house." He put his arm around his son and pulled him close. "I've got a job lined up. I just have to call the man. I'll do it when I get home. Now you tell me why you were on the West Side."

"I had a chance to make some money. I thought we could put it toward the mortgage and you'd feel better."

Scott felt guilt weighting down his chest. "How were you going to make money?"

"When I got to school today I heard one of the high school kids saying he needed somebody to pick something up for him and he would pay fifty bucks. He said he would drive me there, wait in his car and pay me as soon as I came back with his package."

"Billy, I appreciate you trying to help but don't ever do that again. Who was the kid?"

"I don't know his name. Just seen him around school. I was only trying to help out."

"Did you get the package?"

"No. As soon as I got out of the car, the kid pulled away, left me there. That cop pulled up and told me you were looking for me. He took me in his police car. I rode in the back seat, behind the cage. That was scary. He called your cell but you didn't answer. How did you know I was out there?"

Scott parked in front of St. Mary's. "I've got friends that watch out for you and let me know if you might be in trouble. Promise me you won't do that again." He exhaled and looked up at the cross on the church's steeple, *Thank you, God.*

"I promise, Dad."

"I've got to call Father Dugan and let him know about that kid that offered you the money. He'll probably want to talk to you."

"Ok." Billy opened the car door and stepped onto the sidewalk. He looked back through the open window. "I'm sorry, Dad. I was only trying to help." He closed the door and ran into the school.

Richard Volley picked up his phone. "Director of the—"

"Cut the bullshit. It's me," Everson said. "There's a problem. Marchese's dead, heart attack, at the strip club. He had money on him for the Russian. I need you to contact Drazen to make sure he got the cash."

"Why me?"

"Because you owe me. I don't ask for much, but now it's payback time. Twenty grand's gone missing. I need you to get on top of this today." He gave Volley Drazen Ivanov's cell phone number. "Tell him you're calling on behalf of the King and you want to speak to the Bishop."

Volley's phone went silent. He put the receiver down. His desk was flanked by the Stars and Stripes on one side and the Task Force flag on the other. He spun around in his black leather chair and stared at the photos on the wall behind him. The President and Everson back when he was governor. He could feel it. This payback was going to bite him in the ass.

He rubbed a hand across his lips. He'd need a throwaway phone, so that no call to the Russian mobster could be traced to his office. Not one of the throwaways they had on hand, either. *Who do I get to do this?* He turned in his chair and tapped his fingers on his desk. An intern, or whatever they called them. Someone who'd be gone in a couple of months, never to be heard from again. Decision made, he asked his secretary to come into his office.

Margie came in with her steno pad. She was a thick-bodied woman five years from retirement. A hand-me-down from Volley's predecessor, dressed in a gray suit that matched her hair. "Yes, Mr. Volley?"

"Do we still have some of those college kids sitting around here? You know, the ones that are somebody's niece or nephew."

"We have two interns, one young man—I believe the son of an alderman—and one young lady. I think her mother is with the prosecutor's office."

Definitely an alderman's son should know not to talk, Volley thought. "Send the young man in. What's his name?

"James DeYoung. I'll call him right away." Margie returned to her desk.

A few minutes later DeYoung knocked on Volley's door. He was shorter than the director and wore khakis, a white shirt and blue tie that his father must have bought when he was first elected into office thirty years ago.

"Hi, Jimmy." Volley stood. "Come on in…and close the door." He gave the kid a firm handshake. "How's your dad doing? I meant to call him and tell him what a great job you're doing here."

"Thanks, Mr. Volley." The boy scratched the side of his head and furrowed his brow.

"I've a special assignment for you. We need a couple of throw-away phones for an undercover case that's just getting under way, and as luck would have it, we don't have any in inventory." He opened his desk drawer and pulled out $200 in twenties. "Here's some cash from an undercover fund. I'd like you to go out and buy two of those phones."

"Yes, sir. Anything I can do to help."

"Now remember, this is for an official task force undercover investigation. This is very sensitive and I'm counting on the fact that I can trust you. You can't tell anyone about this. Not your girlfriend, your father, not anyone." He handed the cash to DeYoung.

"You can trust me, Mr. Volley." The kid stashed the money in his pants pocket.

"Good." Volley nodded toward the door. "We need them ASAP. Bring them right back to me. If my door is closed, just knock. And remember, not a word to anyone, even in the office. This case is on a need-to-know basis."

"Yes, sir. I'll be back in twenty minutes." DeYoung rushed to door and let himself out.

By nine-thirty a.m., Volley had the phones. He walked past Margie and briefly stopped at her desk. "I have a meeting. Should be back in time for lunch." He left the building, drove in his government-issued Crown Victoria to an empty parking lot at U.S. Cellular Field, and punched in Ivanov's number.

A gravelly voice with a thick accent answered. "Yes?"

"Is this the man from the Pole Club?"

"Who's this?"

"This is an associate of Marchese's. I understand that there was a problem last night."

"I don't know you."

"I was asked to call you by Marchese's superior. Surely you know who I mean."

"I don't know you."

Volley's phone went dead. He stared at it, mouth dry. "How the fuck am I supposed to do this if the fuckin' Russian won't talk to me?" Then he remembered. "Shit, the King and the Bishop. Got to play his game." He dialed the number again.

"Yeah?" Same voice as before.

"It's me—"

"I told you I don't—"

"The King, I'm calling for the King. He wants me to talk to the Bishop."

"Who the fuck are you and why doesn't he call me?"

"I'm just a…just a pawn. The King is being careful. He thought it was better for him and you if I called about that situation. He wanted to know if you got the package from that guy."

"Where are you calling from?"

"I'm on a cell."

"You tell him there was no package."

"The King said the man had a package for you," Volley said.

The voice on the other end hardened. "I don't deal with a pawn. You tell him to come see me personally. Tell him there was no package."

The phone went dead.

Chapter 7

Wednesday, 10:00 AM

MARTI RUBBED HER EYES. HER consciousness came back in pieces. She struggled to open her eyes and blinked at the sunlight that came through the cracks between the garbage bags and the windows. Half of the mattresses were empty. One young white boy was passed out on a mattress next to her. Across from her were two black men and three black women. She took a deep breath, felt the looseness of her jeans and the needle in her skin. She yanked the syringe out, watched a trickle of blood ooze down her arm. Then she looked down. The snap on her jeans was undone and the zipper pulled down.

Marti shoved her hand down her pants, searching for the envelope. It was gone. She tried to right herself and collapsed onto the mattress. She rolled over onto one elbow and shouted, "Old man, where are you? You stole my money."

One of the women on the other side of the room braced her arms behind her and propped herself up, looking at Marti. "Shut up, bitch. If you had any money you wouldn't be here."

"Where is he? The man that gave me the shit last night."

"Ain't no man here. Just us junkies. And junkies ain't got no money. So shut the fuck up and let me go back to sleep." The woman fell back onto the mattress and rolled over, turning her back on Marti.

Marti grabbed the five packets, stuffed them in her pocket, leaned over and shook the white boy.

He stirred and muttered. "What? What is it?"

"Who was the man that was here last night?"

"Don't know. Not always the same guy. Just a junkie like us workin' to get his shit."

Marti curled into a ball, arms wrapped around her knees, her head resting on them. "I'm dead."

Chapter 8

Scott pulled into his garage, grabbed the potato chip bag and walked up the gangway to his house, looking over his shoulder for cops. He entered through the back door, locked it and stepped out of his sticky pants.

He grabbed his wallet from the back pocket, rushed up the back stairs into the kitchen with the potato chip bag in hand, poured a tall glass of water and grabbed three pills out of the bag. He tossed the pills into his mouth. *What the hell am I doing? My kid could have been killed today.*

Scott shook his head, spit the pills into the sink and crushed the bag. He opened the cabinet door under the sink, tossed the bag into the trash can and slammed the door shut. "I got to kick this before something happens I'll regret."

He opened his wallet and found the business card Volley had given him for Everson's law firm. *As much as I regret calling that prick's uncle, I've got to get a job. Can't let the house go. It would crush Billy.* He sat down at the kitchen table and tapped in the number on his cell phone.

"Everson and Associates," a young lady answered.

"My name is Scott Garity. Richard Volley suggested I call Mr. Everson."

"Let me see if he's available."

A few minutes later the husky voice Scott had heard on TV news programs and radio shows announced Everson's presence. "James Everson."

"Mr. Everson, this is Scott Garity. I used to work for your nephew on the federal drug task force. He said you might be looking for an investigator for your firm and suggested I call you."

"As a matter of fact, I am." Scott heard pages turning, likely Everson paging through a calendar. "Let's see, today is Wednesday. Can you come in Friday at ten? I have an assignment I can give you right away. One of our clients could use your services. We can offer you a three thousand dollar retainer and pay you seventy-five an hour. Would that meet your requirements?"

"Yes, sir."

"Good. See you then."

"I'll be there. Thank you, sir." The line went quiet and Scott closed his flip phone.

Three thousand dollars. His eyes flashed to the sink. *I'll have money for the mortgage.* He pushed his hand through his hair and shook his head. He got up, headed toward the living room and stopped, then marched back to the sink, grabbed the loose pills, tossed them into his mouth and downed them with the water. He dropped the glass and it shattered. He folded his arms across the sink and rested his forehead on them as tears welled from his self-betrayal.

Marti wrapped the hypodermic in her sweatshirt and stuffed the dime bags in her back pocket. The dope, syringe, the clothes on her back and the hundred dollars in her pocket were her sole possessions. She wobbled down the stairs of number 206, one hand bracing herself against the wall, the other holding her sweatshirt tight as she came down from the end of her dream world high. She stepped into the foyer and leaned against the wall. An elderly man hobbled past her pushing a broom. Rays of sunlight burst through the bullet holes in the door. She pushed it open, stepped out and shielded her eyes from the bright morning sun.

She doddered down the courtyard sidewalk toward the street past young black men dressed in baggy jeans, jerseys and do-rags. Music screamed at her from open apartment windows, LL Cool J chanting, " Doin' it" from one side and Junior Mafia bellowing, "Get Money" from the other.

One of men stepped in front of her. "Hey, baby, lookin' for company?"

She jabbed her hand against his chest, knocking him out of the way.

He came up by her side and walked next to her, step by step. "Hey, honey, don't do me like that. I gotta job. Not like the rest of these niggers."

She shoved him again.

"You better be careful." He pointed a finger at her. "White girl walking around here be in trouble without a man." He waved his hand at her and turned back toward the building entrance.

A little further down the street, she saw a light-skinned man get out of a shiny black car. His features looked more white than black—small nose and narrow lips and gheri curls running down the back of his neck. Dressed in black, he was doing his best pimp stroll toward her. His shoulders sashayed back and forth in a loose-fitting designer shirt, legs leisurely strutted ahead in Armani slacks, and thousand-dollar shoes floated on the sidewalk. A gold medallion flashed in the sun against his black silk shirt.

"You need a ride outta the hood, sweetie?"

Marti focused on the medallion, a large letter D. "Just tell me how to get out of here and then leave me alone."

"Got me a nice El Do. We put the top down and go cruising."

"Get away from me. I want a cab. Took one here last night."

He shrugged. "Fact be, it ain't gonna happen in this neighborhood. They'll bring you here if you want something, but they don't be crusin' around here looking for a fare."

He reached for her hand. She shook him off. "Don't be touching me."

"Sure, lady. Allow me to introduce myself. My name is DeMarcus." He lifted a gold business card holder out of his shirt pocket, held it between his thumb and index finger, popped it open and handed her a card. "DeMarcus 'De Man' DeWayne. The only for sure way outta here for you is with me." He pointed his thumb at his medallion. 'De Man'."

Don't know where I am or where to go. Her brow furrowed and she tightened her grip on her sweatshirt. "Why are you the only way out of here for me?"

"Respect. I got it. Watch, you come with me to my El Do and it'll be like the Red Sea parting for Moses. Hope you understand the Bible. My daddy be a minister."

He held out his arm. Marti laid her hand on his forearm and they walked to his ride. Boys stepped off the sidewalk onto the hardened dirt as DeMarcus and Marti passed by. He opened the passenger door and she slid into the glistening seat. "Nice car, but it's kind of old."

He stepped around the car and jumped into the front seat. "This ride be a '76 Cadillac El Dorado." He started the engine, released the levers above the windshield, and pushed a button. The convertible top hummed back. "Used to belong to the king of the pimps on the West Side. After he met with an unfortunate accident, I bought it from his estate. This car never seen a winter's day since I owned it. Now, where you want to go? I gotta a crib on the North Side, or I can get you a room in a nice hotel. You can take a nice long bath and relax a little. You a beautiful woman, but you look like you had a tough night."

Why not, Marti thought. She didn't have much choice, after all. "A room would be nice, DeMarcus."

"And while you relaxing, I'll get us some Chinese."

At 11:00 a.m. Ivan unlocked the door to the six-flat and trudged up the three flights of stairs to the dancers' apartment. He heard the music from the Auktyon CD that he'd left in the CD player blasting through the door. *Good, they're awake.*

He shoved the key in the deadbolt and cranked it open. Nataliya stood at the kitchen counter in a black bra and panties, nibbling on a slice of buttered toast. Seeing her in her underwear rather than naked at the club made him feel like they had an intimate relationship. He hurried up to her and put his arm around her shoulders, "Good morning, beautiful. How are you today?"

She put her toast down, shrugged him off and walked into the bedroom as Veronika strolled out in the same jeans and sweatshirt she'd been wearing when he dropped her and the others off six hours ago. Her face was pale, awaiting the makeup she would paint on at the club. She walked past him without a glance of recognition, picked up Nataliya's leftover toast and stuffed it into her mouth. "You better check on the lesbo girl or we'll be late and Marko will slap your face until it's as pink as your ass," she said through a mouthful of food.

Ivan pursed his lips. He went to Tanya's bedroom door, looking over his shoulder as he turned the key in the lock. "Why do you talk to me like that? Why you show me no respect, bitch?"

"You're a bus driver for whores. You can do me no good. I will marry a john one day and leave you all behind. A man like you…." She spit on the floor.

"A bitch like you…." He pushed the door open, and his jaw dropped. "Oh fuck." He rushed to the corner of the room. Tanya lay there, dried vomit covering her lips, staring eyes fixed on the ceiling. He knelt down, grabbed her wrist, and felt for a pulse. Nothing. Her skin was like ice.

Chapter 9

Wednesday, 11:45 PM

James Everson spooned against Jeanie and stroked her blonde hair. "I've got a meeting in a little while. Do you mind if I borrow your car?"

His receptionist rolled over to face him. "Why do you need my car?"

"It's a meeting that requires some discretion."

"Okay, honey. My keys are on the nightstand. How long will you be gone?"

He rolled out of bed, slipped his pants on and stepped into his shoes. "Not long, maybe a half-hour, forty-five minutes. I've got to go home tonight."

She frowned. "You have to go home again. That seems to be happening more often lately. Are you growing tired of me?"

"I have an early appointment with a client on the North Shore, that's all. I'll be back in a little while." He stood up and finished dressing. As he stepped out the door, Jeanie punched her pillow.

Fifteen minutes later, Everson pulled in next to a dark green Lexus parked in an empty grocery store lot ten minutes away from the Pole Club. He pushed the button and his window hummed down. "Hello, Drazen."

The Russian smirked. "The King has a Chevy for a chariot?"

"It belongs to a friend. So where's my money?" Everson asked.

"What money? I never got any money."

"Marchese got the money and he made it to your club. As far as I'm concerned, it was in your hands."

"I see. But you're confused about one thing. The money never got into my hands because your man created such a distraction, one of my whores slipped out the back door. I had a lot of money invested in her. It will cost me thirty thousand dollars to replace her, not to mention the problem it will cause with the other whores."

Everson laughed. "Thirty thousand. Your whores come with the *Good Housekeeping* seal of approval?"

"It's not so funny to me."

"Me either. Your missing whore, what's the chance she took my money?"

"That would be a serious problem for her. It never happened before."

"Was Marchese missing anything else?"

Drazen paused.

"Well?"

Drazen gave a slight nod. "His wallet gone."

"Then your bitch took my money." Everson pointed his finger at the Russian. "Find her and we find my money, and you teach her a lesson so this never happens again."

"Finding her is not easy."

"Does she have a passport?"

"She has no papers," Drazen said.

"She has my twenty thousand bucks. She can get a lot with that. We have to move quickly. You have your people look for her. I have a man coming into my office tomorrow at ten. He has a lot of street contacts. Between your people and this man, we'll find her. Send me a picture of her and anything you know about her first thing tomorrow and we'll take care of this."

Drazen frowned. "Who is this man you think can find her?"

"He's a former federal agent who's been on the street a long time."

"Fuckin' federal agent." Drazen slammed his fist against the steering wheel. "Are you crazy? I'm cleaning your money, running whores and shit you don't even know about, and you want to get a Fed involved."

"Don't worry about him. He can get the job done, and he's been fucked over by the G. He's looking out for himself."

The Russian looked skeptical. "You keep him away from my people and my place or I can't promise he'll be around long enough to find the whore." He curled his hand into the shape of a gun, pointed his forefinger at the former governor and lowered his thumb.

CHAPTER 10

Friday, 2:00 AM

IVAN PULLED THE VAN UP to the rear of the six-flat. He shifted into park, shut off the engine and looked at Marko. "Where are we going to put Tanya?"

Marko took a drag on a joint, held the smoke in his lungs and exhaled. "She's a fucking junkie. We'll take where it won't be a surprise when they find her body."

"Where's that?"

"Where the niggers live, dumbshit."

"Fuck, man, I don't want to get shot in the ghetto."

Marko pulled a Glock 19 from his waistband and waved it in front of Ivan. "I got fifteen rounds in the magazine, one in the chamber and another magazine in my pocket. I could take on the fuckin' Gangster Disciples and have a few rounds left over for the P-Stone Nation."

"What about me? I need something too?"

Marko slipped the Glock into his waistband, leaned forward and pulled a Smith & Wesson Chief's Special from his ankle holster. "Here, put this in your pocket and if you shoot me I'll fuckin' kill you."

Ivan grabbed the revolver. "This is lot smaller than yours."

Marko laughed. "Your dick is a lot smaller than mine, it's not a perfect world."

"How many bullets does this hold?"

"Five."

"What the fuck. I got five bullets and you got—"

"Thirty-five."

"That's not fair. What if we get in trouble? What am I supposed to do?"

"Make sure you save one for yourself, dumbshit. Now get the rug in the back and carry it upstairs. I'm going to finish my joint."

Ivan opened his door, mumbling, "It's not fair. I only got five and you got…" His voice trailed off as he stepped to the back of the van, opened the rear door and pulled out the rolled-up carpet. He tossed it on his skinny shoulders and headed to the rear door of the apartment building.

Marko rolled down his window. "Hurry up, we've got to be back by four to pick up the broads." He opened the door, stepped out and flicked his joint into the air. The embers flew into the night.

Ivan unlocked the rear door of the building and dragged the carpet up the stairs, Marko following. "My old man was pissed Tanya died," Marko said. "I didn't tell him we didn't let her have her fix."

Ivan stopped at the apartment door. "*We*? You—"

"Don't *you* me. You were there." Marko pushed the door open. "You didn't say nothing. Shut the fuck up, get in there and roll her up in the carpet."

They went through the apartment to Tanya's bedroom, where Ivan unlocked the bedroom door, dragged the carpet to the side of the bed and unrolled it. Marko reached into his jacket pocket, pulled out two sets of surgical gloves and tossed a set to Ivan. "Put these on. You grab her by the shoulders. I'll get the legs." They lifted her body, dropped it onto the carpet and rolled it up. "Did the broads say anything?"

"They were stone silent. Looked scared shitless. Didn't say anything in front of me."

"Good. Now they know what could happen if they get out of line. My old man was fuckin' pissed. Bitching that he lost money on her. Paid for her boob job and an abortion." They hefted the carpet onto their shoulders and headed out of the bedroom. As they stepped over the threshold, Ivan stopped and half-turned to stick the key into bedroom door lock.

"What're you doing?" Marko said. "Leave the door open. When we bring the broads back, we want them to see the empty room. It's a good reminder."

Ivan nodded and withdrew the key. "What's he going to do about a new girl?"

"He called the guy in Bosnia. Got three more broads coming in, should be here by Monday. Any of them dogs, he'll sell the whore to a pimp. She'll end up being a streetwalker."

They put Tanya's body in the back of the van and headed to the West Side. By two forty-five they found an empty lot. The weeds were knee high around the carcass of a rusted-out Chevy and empty 55-gallon drums used by the junkies and the homeless to keep warm in the winter. Amid the weeds, trash littered the ground. They looked for anyone that might be watching, but saw nothing. Ivan doused the van's lights, then headed down the block and around to the alley on the back side of the lot. He shoved the gearshift into park. Marko yanked the bulb out of the dome light. They skirted around to the back of the van, took out the loaded carpet and crept to the back of the rusted Chevy with it on their shoulders. They lowered the carpet to chest height, grabbed the edge and let it unroll toward the car. Tanya's body landed with a thud under the trunk.

"Something for the rats to nibble on," Marko said as they plodded back to the van, tossed the empty carpet in and headed back to the club.

Chapter 11

Scott tossed and turned. A recurring dream drifted through the fog in his brain and stole his sleep. He heard his father calling him downstairs into the basement. He visualized his ten-year-old self reluctantly inching down the stairs, a death grip on the railing. His fear mounted as his father's face changed to his own and Billy was the one creeping down the stairs. Scott awoke, sweat pouring down his face. He glanced at the alarm clock on his nightstand. Four a.m. He was broke and had rationed his pills, trying to make them last until he got money from Everson. He'd cut his dosage to fifteen on Wednesday, twelve on Thursday and three for Friday morning. The feeling of a warm bath he got from thirty pills a day had been replaced with anxiety, hyperventilation and night sweats. His mouth was dry and his heart raced. A pain behind his eyes felt as if someone was pounding a nail into his temple.

He lay there until seven o'clock, and then forced himself to shower and dress while he listened to sounds of Billy getting himself off to school. Scott was afraid to face him in his current condition, made worse by remnants of the guilt of his nightmare. After Billy left, he downed his last three Vicodin and headed to his meeting with Everson.

Scott wore his best suit, a double-breasted navy-blue pinstripe off the rack from Sears, a crisp white shirt and a red tie. He arrived at Everson's office on LaSalle Street across from City Hall, paused at the door and took a moment to gather himself by reading the names of the fifteen associates listed under Everson's name on the frosted glass. *Got to keep it together for half an hour and get the money.*

He opened the door and stepped into an office steeped in dark hardwood, beige walls, brown leather and paintings of tall ships. In the center of the reception area was a ship's wheel and compass. To the left was a sliding glass window with a blonde receptionist in her mid-thirties seated behind it.

The window slid open. "May I help you?" she said.

Scott walked toward her. "Scott Garity, I have a ten o'clock with Mr. Everson." He glanced at her name plate and the photograph on her desk of two young girls.

"I'll let him know you're here. Please take a seat, Mr. Garity."

"Thanks, Jeanie. Your girls?"

"Yes." She glanced at the photo and smiled. "They're eleven and nine."

"They're beautiful." He nodded and walked over to the sofa. He sank into the deep, soft leather and skimmed through a copy of *Sailing Magazine* on the coffee table in front of him.

A few minutes later, the door to the inner sanctum opened, revealing James Everson, three inches taller than Scott, a solid 230 pounds and in his late sixties. His gray hair was thinning on top but he was still bigger in real life than Scott had imagined. "Hi, Scott." Everson waved his arm. "Come on in."

Scott dropped the magazine back on the coffee table and marched up to Everson. He reached out and received a bone-crushing handshake. "Pleasure to meet you, Governor." He looked at the man's charcoal gray suit. *Scott, he must think we're long lost buddies. His damn suit probably cost twice my mortgage payment.*

"Please, that's ancient history. Call me Jim and come on down. I'm in the corner office." He waved Scott ahead. "Jeanie, get us a couple of coffees. Scott, how do like yours?"

"Cream and sugar, please."

They walked past seven doors, a secretary in front of each one with the name of an associate listed in gold letters on each door. At the door to Everson's office, the corridor took a ninety-degree bend. The offices of the remaining associates ran the length of the hallway. Scott walked into the office and Everson closed the door behind them. The office had windows on two sides. The remaining two walls were covered with maritime paintings like the ones in the lobby. The former governor's large mahogany desk filled one corner. Scott sat in one of the two leather chairs in front of the desk. "I didn't know you were into boats."

Everson pointed to a picture on the wall behind Scott. "That's my baby, the *Katherine*, thirty-three foot Hunter. Had to name it after the wife or there would be no peace. Keep her in Monroe Harbor. Any chance I get, I sneak out of the office and take her for a sail. Nothing like being out on the lake. You ever try it?"

"No, never been sailing. Gone fishing a few times on charters."

There was a knock on the door and Jeanie stepped in with two mugs of coffee and a couple of cheese Danish on a tray. She set it on the corner of Everson's desk and left the office closing the door behind her.

Everson grabbed a cup and took a sip. "We'll have to get you out there. Richard told me about your situation. Damn shame. You put your life on the line, catch a bullet for them, and they can't keep you on the job."

"Richard said in twelve months I can apply for reinstatement." Scott took the remaining mug off the tray. His hand started to tremble, so he wrapped his other hand around it and held the mug in his lap.

"Let's see if we can keep you busy until then." Everson opened his center desk drawer, removed an envelope and dumped the contents onto his desk. "I hope you don't mind, but I took the liberty of getting some of your personal information from Richard so we could expedite things. I still know a few people in the state building. Got you a private investigator's license. If the situation calls for it, the license will allow you to carry a firearm. I know you feds like to pack."

Scott reached for the license and looked at the photo, which was a copy of the picture that was on his task force credentials. "You do fast work. This case you want me to work on, what's it involve?"

"Our client base is international. One of our client's daughters came here from Europe. She was going to go to school here, but somewhere along the line got hooked up with the wrong people. Last we know, she was an exotic dancer. She disappeared last Tuesday night."

Everson pulled out a second envelope, letter size, with a clasp on it. He opened it and slid the contents, a portrait-size photograph and a roll of hundred-dollar bills, onto his desk. He handed the photo to Scott. It was a full nude body shot of a young woman sitting on a stool, her back facing the photographer. Beneath her short platinum hair, a dragon tattoo covered her back and its tail crawled down her leg. In the upper right hand corner of the photograph was scrawled the name *Marti*.

"She really got into the life," Scott said.

"The good thing is, she hasn't been gone long. She was, shall we say, tending to a customer's needs in the VIP room at a club. The guy had a heart attack and died." Everson lifted a cigar from a humidor on his desk, clipped the end and placed the cigar between his lips. "She took whatever he had and walked out. No such thing as safe sex anymore." The ex-governor laughed and pushed the roll of greenbacks toward Scott. "Here's your retainer. Keep track of your hours. When this is depleted, let me know and we'll get you more. You do well and you can become my main man. The governor's man," he said with a smirk. "And make a lot of money."

Scott put the mug on the tray, reached for the cash and slipped it into his inside suit coat pocket. "Which club was it?"

"The owner is cooperating with us but doesn't want this going public. You can understand that he doesn't want something like this getting out. Bad publicity. So I promised him I wouldn't disclose the club to you. If you have any questions for him, give them to me and I'll get the answers for you."

What am I getting into, Scott wondered. "Who was the customer?"

Everson hesitated. "I'm not trying to be uncooperative. He was a political figure and married, so we have to be sensitive about that too."

Scott ran a hand across his lips. "Well, if he had any credit cards, she's probably using them. Those could be some good leads."

"He didn't have any credit cards. This fellow only used cash."

"Do we know how much cash he had?"

"He typically carried several thousand dollars."

Scott nodded. "So she could have enough money to do just about anything. Even fly back to Europe."

"No, she's undocumented."

"Does she have an address?"

"Don't have one for her."

Scott nodded again. *Everson's client is from Europe. Their daughter comes into the country without documents. Something's out of sync here. But I'll take the money and run. I can be the governor's man, at least for a while.* "Okay, I think I've got the picture. Let me get to work. I'll keep you informed if anything comes up." He pushed himself out of the chair. "Oh, one more question. What's her full name?"

"Martina Zicek," Everson said. "They call her Marti."

Chapter 12

Everson walked with Garity to the lobby and wished him luck. He returned to his office, sat in his chair and gazed out the window at the skyline. *Garity asked a lot of questions. He might find out more than he needs to know. Better check the other accounts Marchese set up.* He unlocked the right-hand desk drawer and removed a 3x5 card listing four banks, account names and numbers, and their PIN numbers.

He punched in the telephone number for the first bank's automated response system, hit the keys identifying the account number and PIN number, listened to his options, and punched two for the last five transactions.

The artificially soothing computerized voice gave him the bad news. "The last five transactions during the preceding seven-day period were an ATM withdrawal of five hundred dollars on September 11, an ATM withdrawal of five hundred dollars on September 11, and an ATM withdrawal of five hundred dollars on September 11. There were no other transactions during this period."

Everson slammed the receiver down. "Son of a bitch." *That whore stole more than the twenty thousand.* He picked up his phone and went through the same process with the remaining three banks, and found the same result. *Six grand on top of the twenty thousand she stole.* He pressed the button for the office intercom. "Get in here," he told Jeanie when she answered.

Everson heard her heels clicking on the wood floor, almost at a run. She stepped into his office.

"Close the damn door," he said.

Jeanie pushed it shut until she heard the lock click. She turned to face him. "What's wrong, James?"

"Money's missing from the special accounts. The ones Marchese held for me. I want you to close those accounts and transfer the balances to new accounts. We've got some old corporations that were set up years ago. Use those charters if the banks need them."

"What if the banks won't close the accounts? Marchese's was the only signature on them."

"Jesus, Jeanie. Do you think I'm stupid? There's a signed power of attorney in his client file."

She blanched. "I'm sorry. I didn't know. I'm just—"

"Go now! Before that bitch steals any more money from me."

Her forehead furrowed. "What bitch?"

Everson pointed at the door. "Go."

Scott walked to the parking garage around the corner from Everson's office. Tossed his suit coat and tie into the trunk and of his Oldsmobile and pointed it westbound on the Eisenhower Expressway. The late morning traffic was light and in fifteen minutes he exited at Laramie Avenue. He spent the rest of the morning dispersing his new fortune: a thousand dollars to his pusher, who gave him 150 pills for the large-volume purchase, and eight hundred to his banker to get his mortgage up to date. That left him with twelve hundred bucks of folding money in his pocket.

Marti woke up and stretched her arms and legs in the king-sized bed. The silk sheets and pillow cases caressed her body. She rolled over, grabbed the bottle of Cristal in the ice bucket and poured the last ounces into her champagne glass. She swallowed it and felt the bubbles tickling her throat. She looked at DeMarcus, who was in a deep sleep. "Thank you for the best three days of my life," she whispered.

She stepped out of bed, slipped on the white bathrobe furnished by the hotel that lay at the foot of the bed, and walked to the closet. She flicked through the clothes they had spent the better part of Thursday buying on the Gold Coast. Then she strolled into the bathroom and looked at her reflection. Her harsh platinum hair was now a soft honey color, her matching manicure and pedicure a delicate ivory. Her eyes filled with tears of joy. *Finally, I'm living my dream.*

She heard footsteps approaching the bathroom. The door opened and DeMarcus stood there, holding her worn jeans and sweatshirt over one arm and four dime bags in his right palm. "What's this shit?" He dropped her clothes to the floor, lifted the toilet seat, and tossed the bags into the bowl.

"God damn it. What the fuck." Marti fell to her knees and dipped her hands into the water.

He flushed the toilet, grabbed her by the collar of her robe and yanked her up.

She shook out of the robe and stood naked, watching the tinfoil packets swirl around the toilet and disappear. "You fucker, I need my shit."

"You don't need that brown Mexican skag. I'll get you white Asian smack that's so good you don't have to shoot it up. You put a dab on your finger, rub it on your gums and you'll be in heaven. You'll never have to worry about a needle again."

She fell into his arms repeating to herself, *the best three days of my life.*

Chapter 13

Friday, 9:00 PM

SCOTT SAT ON THE EDGE of Billy's bed. "I want you to know I paid the mortgage today, so you don't have to worry about the bank taking the house away from us."

Billy leaned back against his pillow. "Thanks, Dad."

"And like we talked about, you don't have to do anything to help pay the mortgage. You just focus on being a twelve-year-old."

"So you've got a new job?"

Scott pulled his private investigator's identification card out of his pocket and handed it to his son. "I'm a private eye. Just like the guys you see on TV."

"It looks just like your fed ID."

Scott grinned. "Going to go to work tonight, just like when I was a fed. Doing surveillance. I'm going to be late, so Father Dugan will spend the night with you."

"Can I stay up with him and watch TV?"

The doorbell rang and Billy scrambled out of bed. "I'll let him in," he called as he ran down the stairs. Scott followed.

Billy opened the door. The old family priest stood there, balancing two paper bags on top of a pizza box. "Father Dugan, can we stay up late and watch TV? Dad said it was up to you."

"Oh, laddie, if it was up to me we'd stay up all night, but my tired old body and mind have other ideas. You know, birthday number seventy-two is coming up in a few months." The priest's face was lined with cracks like an old prune and thin red veins crossed his nose like interstate highways on a map. He handed the box and bags to Billy, and the boy ran into the kitchen.

Father Dugan cocked his head. "Scottie, why didn't you tell me the boy wanted to stay up? I brought a couple of porno tapes and a bottle of Irish Rose."

Scott grimaced.

"Hey, Dad, Father Dugan brought *Toy Story* and *Batman Forever*. I wanna watch *Batman*." He ran to the living room and shoved the tape into the VCR. "Can I start the movie?"

"Go ahead." Scott shook his head at Father Dugan. "Pornos, you bullshitter. Let's go into the kitchen and get some plates."

Dugan followed Scott. "Well, I hope you've got a date tonight. It's about time for Billy to have a female's influence."

"I'm going to see several females tonight—at a strip club."

Dugan's eyebrows shot to the ceiling. "You'll certainly find some ladies there that will be excellent candidates for step-motherhood."

Scott handed the priest his new ID, then pulled three plates out of a cabinet.

Dugan looked the license over. "Private investigator? Don't tell me someone is paying you for this escapade."

"Like they say, it's a tough job but somebody's got to do it. Actually, they don't want me to do this. But it seems like the client doesn't want me to do something that's so logical, it makes me wonder. So I'm going to do it."

"Sounds like you, doing what your boss tells you not to. Who is this guy?"

"Our former governor, James Everson."

Dugan shook his head. "Jesus Christ, the governor. Don't piss him off. He's got a reputation for crushing people that cross him. What are you working on?"

"One of his client's daughters has gone astray." Scott distributed slices of pizza onto the plates, while Father Dugan lifted a two-liter bottle of Dr. Pepper out of a bag and poured it into glasses. "She was supposed to be going to school, got involved with the wrong crowd, got a job as an exotic dancer and disappeared last Tuesday. So I'm looking for her."

"What are you going to do if you find her?"

"Give the gov a big bill. Any more questions? If not, I got a hungry boy out there." They headed for the living room, carrying the pizza and pops. Scott downed two slices and his soda. "I better head out. You boys behave yourselves and don't stay up too late."

Father Dugan cleared his throat, looked at Scott and cocked his head.

Scott parked across the street from the Pole Club at ten-thirty. The parking lot was jammed and there was a steady stream of men entering the joint. He pulled out his binoculars and dictated the license plate numbers he could see into a tape recorder. Marti could be with one of the customers, willingly or not.

He sat in the same place for about an hour and noticed a local squad car slowly ride past him a couple of times. He recorded the squad's tags. *Better move from here. Cruise through the back and pull a few plates.* Scott found a spot in the alley north of the club where he could catch any activity and dictated the tag numbers from a black Mercedes, a dark green Lexus and several other vehicles into his tape recorder.

At midnight the club's rear door opened. A motion detector triggered the light over the door as a thick-bodied young man stepped out with a cigarette dangling from his mouth. The man paced back and forth. After a couple of minutes, the headlights of a car shone on him as it turned into the rear parking lot from the south side of the building. The car stopped at his side. The young man handed an envelope to the driver, said a few words and then re-entered the club. The car headed up the alley toward Scott and then past him as he sunk in the driver's seat. *It's the same squad that checked me out on the street.*

Scott straightened up and started his car. Time to see what was going on inside. He drove around the building and parked underneath the silhouette of the naked woman with one leg wrapped around a pole.

Father Dugan woke with a start and lifted his head from the sofa cushion. Sitting on the floor nearby was Billy. His head rested on Father Dugan's knee. The priest blinked, shook his head and looked at the television. The screen was white. He tapped Billy's shoulder. "Wake up, the movie's over." The priest stretched his arms and yawned. "That was a good flick."

"Father, you fell asleep twenty minutes after it started."

"No I didn't, you did. Go ahead, ask me a question about Batman." He rubbed his eyes and glanced at his watch. "Oh, my gosh, look at the time. You better get ready for bed."

Billy pushed himself up off the floor, "Don't you want me to ask you a question?"

"Don't be sassing me. You go upstairs and get ready for bed." He patted the sofa cushions. "I'll sleep down here. Good night, Billy." He kicked off his shoes and lay down. *See what time his father gets home.*

"Good night, Father. Thanks for the movies and the pizza." Billy ran up the stairs. A short while later, Father Dugan heard water running in the sink and the toilet flushing.

"Good night, Father," Billy yelled from upstairs.

"Finally, now I can get me a little sleepin' aid and something to quench my thirst." He swung his feet into the floor and tiptoed into the kitchen. In the third kitchen cabinet he opened, he found a bottle of Jameson's among several other possibilities. "Ah, that's my boy, a good

Irish whiskey." He lifted the bottle out of the cabinet. A potato chip bag fell from behind it. Father Dugan grinned. "A midnight snack." He grabbed a glass out of the drying rack, unscrewed the cap off the whiskey and poured three fingers into the glass. He took a sip and felt the warmth of it run down his throat and into his stomach. "Thank you, God. I don't think You rested on the seventh day. You made whiskey." He took another sip, put the glass down and reached for the potato chip bag. *Feels heavy.* He opened the bag and looked inside. "Oh, Scottie, what're you doing now?"

Scott weaved between the cars into the entryway, where two men waited. They wore badges on their belts and black Pole Club T-shirts with the naked woman from the sign emblazoned on them. Off-duty cops moonlighting as security.

"Five bucks cover charge, sir," one cop said.

Scott pulled a roll of cash from his pocket and handed the cop a five. "Looks like a full house. Could barely get a parking spot."

The other cop approached him, "Can you raise your arms for a pat-down, sir?"

He lifted his arms over his head and the cop brushed his hands down Scott's torso. "Okay, go ahead," he said, and waved him in.

The music blasted as three girls wearing G-strings and garters pranced from backstage onto the bar, approaching a set of brass poles. A voice over the PA system interrupted the music. "Gentlemen, introducing three of the most beautiful women directly from Europe. The sexy blonde, Veronika, from Sweden." The blonde bowed. "The lovely brunette from Warsaw, Nataliya." A pirouette followed this one's introduction. "And starring at the center pole, our redhead Olga, who just arrived from Moscow." Olga jumped toward her pole in the center of the bar and struck a pose.

The music began thumping. The crowd, three deep at the bar and tables full of patrons, gave a standing ovation. Red, green and blue lights flashed off the girls' bodies as they gyrated around the poles. Lasers shot green beams that danced with the music.

A waitress approached Scott. "Hi, sweetheart, can I get you a drink?"

"Scotch and water." Scott checked out her red pasties while pretending not to notice.

"That's sixteen dollars for a two-drink minimum."

He pulled a twenty from his roll. "Keep the change." He watched her G-string as she sashayed away.

Scott checked out the bouncers. At least four of them dressed all in black, sport coats, slacks and T-shirts. They all had a distinctive European look about them, along with the physical attributes of National Football League linemen.

One bouncer stayed near the entrance of what Scott figured was the VIP room, allowing clients in and out. Two more circulated around the club dealing with customers who wanted too much from a dancer but didn't want to pay for it. The fourth bouncer remained at the club entrance, watching over the entire operation. Every so often they spoke into microphones at their wrists and received transmissions through the earpieces they wore.

Scott watched one man that was out of uniform. *Looks like the one that gave the envelope to the cops.* He was bulky, thirtyish, wore a black long-sleeved shirt and periodically conferred with an older man who stepped out from a door on the left side of the bar that had a "Private" sign above it. Occasionally he went over and spoke to a bouncer, but never within earshot.

Scott nursed his drinks for a couple of hours, watched the customers and dancers, had a second round but left it untouched, and left the club at three-thirty a.m. *See where the girls go at closing time. One of them might lead me to Marti.*

He parked his car on the south side of the street just south of the club. Better not park in the same spot in case the cops came back for a late-night treat. He slid into the front passenger seat, leaned his back against the door and rested his feet on the driver's seat, watching the club through the driver's-side window. He yawned as time slowly passed. Finally, a van turned into the back parking lot from the north side of the building and braked at the rear door. Scott glanced at his watch. Four twenty-five a.m. A thin man in a T-shirt and jeans hopped out and entered the club. As the rear light flashed on, Scott slid into the driver's seat.

Ten minutes later, the same man exited the rear door. Six girls followed him. They all hopped into the van, which sat there for five minutes. The club door opened again and the cone of light over it fell on the same bulky, thirty-ish guy Scott had seen floating from one bouncer to another, and who'd passed the envelope off to the cops in the alley. *Must be the guy in charge.*

Bulky Guy went to the driver's side of the van, exchanged a few words with somebody there and then walked over to a Mercedes. The van drove to the end of the building and turned toward the front, through the parking lot and north on Mannheim Road. The Mercedes followed.

Scott started the engine, made a U-turn and followed the vehicles. They went north a few miles and turned east. Two blocks later they turned in behind a group of six-flats. Scott went past the one where they'd pulled up, parked in the back two buildings down, and brought his binoculars to his eyes. He watched the girls march out of the van and stand at the back door of the building. The van driver opened it, and they paraded into the building. The man from the Mercedes followed.

The door closed and lights went on in the third floor windows. They had burglar bars, Scott noted. *It's like a prison. No wonder Marti left.* By five a.m. the lights were off and the two men had gotten back in their vehicles. The van headed east and the Mercedes headed north onto Interstate 294. Scott followed the Mercedes for twenty-five minutes, exited east on Willow Road and drove for two miles through village streets bordered by huge houses with deep manicured front yards. The street narrowed and the yards grew so heavily wooded that the houses were no longer visible.

Aware that his was now the only car on the road besides the Mercedes, Scott doused his headlights to avoid detection. The black sedan stopped at Sheridan Road, turned south and halted in front of a wrought iron gate. The gate slowly opened and the Mercedes pulled into a long driveway. Its brake lights lit up the circular drive in front of a three-story mansion. Exterior accent lights revealed a massive wooden front door. The brake lights went off. The driver got out of the car, stood in front of the door for a moment and then entered.

Scott rolled a window down. He could smell the lake air. *In all the cases I worked, I never followed anyone to a North Shore mansion. Who is this guy?*

Chapter 14

Saturday, 6:00 AM

Scott pulled into his garage, left his car and dragged his feet to the back door of his house. He unlocked the door, stepped in, softly closed the door behind him, took his shoes off and tiptoed into the kitchen. He had been awake for almost twenty-four hours and was tired but wired. The one-man surveillance to Winnetka had frayed his nerves, and his doubts about what he was getting into made him wonder if he was overstepping his reach. *Maybe this is too much for one man.*

In years past, he would automatically have known what to do. Now it seemed like he was following a ball of yarn that had unraveled to a single thread and he was at the end of the string. Was it the time off? Had he lost his edge? Or had he acquired fear—the kind of fear when a near-death experience sinks into you?

The morning sky cast a dull light through the kitchen window and raindrops started drumming against the glass. His mouth felt dry and his heart raced. He pulled a glass from the drying rack next to the sink and placed it on the counter. He opened the kitchen cabinet door, grabbed the bottle of Jameson's and looked for the potato chip bag. It wasn't there. He rubbed his chin. *I'm sure I put it there. Maybe it's in my nightstand.* He poured three fingers of the amber liquid into the glass, brought it to his lips and felt the warmth run down his throat as he drank. *A handful of pills for a chaser and I'll be fine.*

Glass in hand, he turned to head upstairs.

Father Dugan blocked the way, leaning against the threshold of the doorway between the kitchen and the living room, hands clasped behind his back. "Breakfast of champions. Guess you need it after a long night of staring at tits and ass."

"I told you it was a job." Scott stepped toward the doorway. "Have a good movie night?"

"You sure one glass is enough to calm your nerves? You're probably jacked up."

"What's got into you? It was a job. I wasn't out chasing tail. The joint closed at four. Then I followed a couple of employees taking the girls to an apartment, which looked like a prison, and from there I followed one of the guys to a mansion in Winnetka. So, boss, I've accounted for all of my time. You mind if I get some sleep now?"

"I never doubted you were working, Scotty. I believe you." Dugan exhaled. "I apologize if I seem difficult. You see, I'm wondering what the hell these are for." He straightened up and brought his right hand from behind his back. In it was the potato chip bag.

Scott knew the whiskey wasn't enough. He needed what was in that bag. He licked his lips. "It was the pain. I couldn't take it and now I'm stuck. I've got to have those."

He reached for the bag. Dugan pulled it back. "You've got to get off these. Where'd you buy these, anyway? They weren't in a prescription bottle."

"My prescription ran out." Scott glanced down. "Bought them on the street."

"Scott, you could have been arrested. What would happen to Billy then?"

"I know. I know. I'm gonna get off of them. It's just going to take some time. Let me have that. I...I just want to take a few."

"No, Scott. You've gotta stop."

"Gimme that." He reached for the bag and tried to yank it out of Dugan's hand. It ripped open. The pills scattered across the floor. Scott fell to his hands and knees, grabbed a handful of pills, tossed them into his mouth and downed them with the whiskey.

"Get up," Dugan said.

Scott leaned back on his haunches.

Billy stepped from behind Father Dugan. "What're you doing, Dad?"

"I've got to pick up these pills, Billy. These are pills I got after I was hurt to kill the pain."

"I'll help you." Billy got down next to his father and scooped up a handful of pills.

Father Dugan knelt too, and the three of them picked up the pills and dropped them into the potato chip bag. "I'll take the bag," Dugan said. "Scott, I want you to visit me this afternoon at the rectory. Three o'clock."

Scott looked into the priest's green eyes and thought, *I need to get more pills.*

Chapter 15

Saturday, October 5, 2:00 PM

SCOTT WOKE TO THE SOUND of Billy cheering on the Yankees in the fourth game of the American League playoffs. He hung his feet over the side of the bed and slipped into a sweatshirt, jogging shorts, socks and New Balance running shoes. *Need a run to work off this rough edge.* He yanked the nightstand drawer open and glanced at his wallet, with the $1,100 cash left over from his retainer. He grabbed $200, stuffed it in his socks, went to the bathroom, splashed his face with water and went downstairs.

"What's happening in the game?" he asked his son.

"Bernie Williams smacked a home run to tie it," Billy said.

Scott propped his right heel on the back of the sofa and bent over, stretching his hamstring. "Damn Yankees always win. One of these years the White Sox will make it to the World Series."

Billy laughed. "Don't hold your breath."

"Come on, you've got to root for the home team, son." He switched legs and stretched his left hamstring.

"Cubs or White Sox? I'll be an old man before either of them makes it to the series."

"Oh yeah? I bet you a Coke the Yankees lose."

"You're on, and let's add a trip to McDonald's for a quarter pounder and fries."

Scott grinned. "I'm heading out to work up an appetite. I hope you saved your allowance. See you later."

"Dad, don't forget you're supposed to meet Father Dugan at three."

"Oh yeah, thanks. I'll be back in time." Scott left the house and jogged east through the residential neighborhood heading toward Columbus Park, the border between the West Side of Chicago and Oak Park.

He started with a slow jog for ten minutes to warm up and then gradually kicked up his speed. Sweat broke across his forehead and rolled down the side of his face. As his speed increased, he breathed through his mouth and his lungs labored for his next breath. For the next ten minutes his quadriceps burned. Then he stopped and leaned over, placed his hands on his knees, his chest expanding and contracting with each breath. He had reached Columbus Park, where he saw young men hovering around the backstops of the baseball fields. He casually went by them, exchanging the $200 for a small plastic bag with twenty-five pills, and slipped the bag inside his sock where the money had been.

It was almost three by time he returned home. As he stepped in the door, he heard Billy say, "You owe me a trip to McDonald's. Yanks won. And you're going to be late for Father Dugan."

"I almost forgot. I got so into my run, I lost track of time. I'll towel off and get right over there." Scott rushed to the upstairs bath, filled a glass with water and downed three pills. He toweled off the sweat from his run, put on a warm-up suit and headed out to his car. *I wonder what Dugan wants—probably to give me a lecture.*

At three-twenty, Scott walked into St. Mary's rectory. Father Dugan's office was the first one down the hallway on the right. The door was open and the priest sat at an oak desk that was older than he was. Dugan closed the magazine he was reading and glanced at his watch. "You're late."

"Sorry, I went for a jog and lost track of time."

As Scott grabbed the back of a wooden armchair in front of the desk, Dugan steepled his hands together and asked, "Are you still seeing the therapist?"

Scott had contemplated sitting down, but after hearing the uncomfortable question just leaned against the chair instead. "I had to stop for a while. My insurance ran out and I couldn't afford it on my disability."

"So now that you're working again, you can swing the treatments?"

"Sure, I can do that. Is that why you wanted to see me? Could have discussed this over the tel—"

"No. Follow me." Father Dugan pushed himself away from the desk, stood, and walked into the hallway and up the stairs. After a moment he looked over his shoulder at Scott, who was trailing him. "I was hoping you'd be on time so you could have been here from the beginning."

"Beginning of what?"

Dugan reached the top of the stairs, where he turned and faced a closed door. Taped to the door was a sheet of paper with "N.A. Meeting" written on it in black magic marker. "The people in here are from all walks of life—banker, lawyer, nurse, homeless and more, and they all have the same problem you do," Dugan said. He knocked on the door, opened it, pushed Scott in and closed the door behind him.

Scott stumbled into the room. His face reddened with anger. *What the hell was Dugan trying to do?* The room was crowded, people scuttling about, looking for chairs. A Hispanic man, olive colored skin and a thin mustache pointing and giving orders.

The man approached Scott and put his hand on Scott's shoulder. "I'm Jorge. Welcome to narcotics anonymous." He pointed to a vacant chair, one of thirteen surrounding a round table. "Father Dugan said we might have a new member joining us." Jorge closed the door.

Scott went to the chair and sat.

"Let me tell you how we do things here," Jorge said. "First of all, whatever is said here, stays here. Your only requirement for membership is a desire to stop using drugs. We go by our first names only unless you develop a relationship with one of us as a sponsor. A sponsor is someone you can call when you think you can't cope and you feel the urge to use. This is a fellowship of men and women who share their experience, strength and hope with each other to help recover from a drug problem. Do you have any questions?"

Scott looked at the people seated around the table. He was sure he could pick out the banker, the lawyer and the homeless man—the white shirts and ties versus the three-day-old stubble and worn-out eyes. But some of others didn't fit. One woman looked like someone's grandmother, another lady could have been a clerk at Marshall Fields.

"Would you like to tell us your name?" Jorge asked.

Scott swallowed. "Do I have to?"

"No, but it's a good way to start."

He could feel beads of sweat rolling down his torso. "Scott."

"Scott, would you like to share?"

Scott squirmed in his seat. *Share, I don't even know what I'm doing here.* He pursed his lips, shook his head and blurted out, "No."

"Sure. Anyone else care to talk?"

There was a brief silence. Then one of the men in a white shirt and tie raised his hand. "My name is Andy and I'm an addict."

"Hi, Andy," the group responded, except for Scott.

"As many of you know, this is my third attempt at recovery. I've been clean for ten days. But I almost slipped today at work. I found an old baggie in my suit pocket and I rushed to the john. I was so desperate I was going lick the dust out of the bag or stick my nose in it. When I got in the bathroom I looked in the mirror and thought of my wife—ex-wife—and how much I've lost." He exhaled, lowered his head and sniffled. "I want her back, but she's dating someone now. They're getting serious. I called her a couple of nights ago. She told me it would be best if I didn't call again. I guess that's all I have to say. Thanks."

"Thank you, Andy," the group responded.

Scott didn't say anything. He glanced at his watch. Four p. m. He guessed he'd be stuck here awhile.

The meeting went on with more of the same until four-thirty, when Jorge called it to a close. "It's time to finish. We'll pass the basket. As always, contributions are not required, but are appreciated." To Scott, he said, "There's no membership fee. Any contributions goes to the coffee and cookie fund. Scott, why don't you take these?" He slid a pamphlet across the table. "We meet every Tuesday and Thursday night at seven, and Saturday and Sunday at three. You're welcome to join us any time. That pamphlet has a list of all the N.A. meetings in the Chicago area. You can attend any one at any time."

Scott hurried out the door leaving the pamphlet on the table.

Chapter 16

Saturday, 9:00 PM

MARTI SLID INTO THE PASSENGER seat of the El Dorado. "I'm nervous, DeMarcus."

DeMarcus put the key in the ignition, started the engine, and headed east on Balmoral Avenue to Sheridan Road, then turned south. He glanced at her and then looked back at the oncoming traffic.

She wore what the saleswoman called, "a little black dress suitable for all occasions." He examined her from top to bottom. The V-shaped neckline accentuated her cleavage. The dress was snug around her waist. Her legs were crossed at her knees. The dress stopped at mid-thigh, revealing the stays of her garter belt at the top of opaque hose. She wore black stiletto heels. He shook his head. "Honey, I wanna take you back home and make love to you all night, but that wouldn't make the boss-lady happy."

"I know, I've got to work to earn my keep."

"You know I'll always be there for you, buy you the things you want and protect you in every way."

She leaned over and kissed his cheek. "That is so important to me, to know that I don't have to worry about anyone hurting me."

"This ain't gonna be like before with those drunken slobs at that club. You're dealing with respectable men—men of position. They gonna tip you nice and you can give half of that to me for the special care I give you. Don't forget, baby, to these men you're Mercedes, not Marti."

"Of course." Marti smiled and massaged the back of his neck, and thought, *tips to you, not.*

"You know you're my main woman. Those others don't compare with you. My feelings for you are special."

"I know that, DeMarcus," *And you can bet as soon as I have enough money saved up to get myself off smack I'm gone.*

DeMarcus braked the El Dorado at the curb of the Gold Coast hotel.

Marti raised her hand. "Look at me shaking. I'm nervous. It's like the first time doing this for you and I don't want to mess up."

DeMarcus stretched his arm across the back of the bucket seats. "You'll be perfect. Old Leland Grayson won't want to let you go. All you gots to do is be yourself and do your thing. Everything else is taken care of. You ain't got to take payment from him. It's all paid for through the escort service. He makes a check payable to the boss lady's business or charges it." DeMarcus chuckled. "Probably deducts it as an entertainment expense on his company's taxes. Like buyin' some client lunch. And I'm sure Leland will give you a nice tip. Go on now, Suite 1103."

Marti took a deep breath and exhaled.

Her door swung open and a doorman dressed in a red waist-length jacket with matching pants and hat extended his hand to her. "Allow me."

DeMarcus kissed her cheek. "I'll be here at eleven. Don't be late, because you have another date at midnight."

She nodded, put one hand in the doorman's, clutched her little black purse in the other and stepped out of the El Dorado. She knew the doorman was eyeing her. The black dress molded to her body swayed with every shift of her hips.

Marti entered the lobby and stood there in amazement. Intimidated by the most beautiful place she had ever seen. The marble floor shone like polished glass. In the center was a round table with a vase as tall as she was, filled with dozens of white roses. The ceiling was thirty-feet high and painted with white and blue clouds interspersed with angels playing golden harps.

"May I help you, madame?" asked a porter in a red uniform.

"Oh, no thank you. I'm meeting a friend." She looked for the elevators and saw the doors on the other side of the roses. She strutted over to the elevators and waited for the wood-paneled doors to open. With a ping they separated, and a group of men in expensive suits stepped out. They held the doors open for her with admiring looks.

Marti exited at the eleventh floor and walked down a blue oriental runner to a black door with the gold numbers 1103. She knocked, and after a moment it opened.

"Hello, dear." The man in the doorway was tall, sixtyish with gray hair combed back and wavy just above his ears. He held a martini glass in one hand and waved her into the room with the other. "Mercedes, is that correct?"

"Yes, Mr. Grayson." She noticed the Rolex he wore, with diamonds circling the bezel, protruding from French cuffs locked together by gold cufflinks.

"Please, call me Leland." He closed the door and locked it.

She stepped to the center of the suite. The sitting area was furnished in contemporary style, with a black leather sofa fronted by a matching coffee table near the windows. She walked behind the sofa and looked at the headlights from the traffic heading up and down Michigan Avenue.

He set his drink on the coffee table, stepped behind her, and placed his hand on her shoulder. "This is a beautiful city. Have you lived here long?"

"No, only a few years. I've never have had the opportunity to see much of it."

"I detect a little bit of a European accent."

"I was born in Chisinau." She felt him pull down the zipper on the back of her dress. His fingers caressed her neck, slid to her shoulders. Her gown fell to the floor.

"Interesting artwork you have here." He traced the head of the dragon tattoo with his forefinger and kissed the back of her neck.

Her shoulders twitched. She turned and looked into Leland's green eyes, noticing for the first time the deep crow's feet in the corners. He grabbed her hand and led her from the living room into the bedroom, where he released her. He sat on the edge of the king-sized bed, smoothed his hair with his fingers, kicked off his shoes and removed his navy slacks. He patted the bed.

Marti dropped her bra to the floor. Wearing only her garter belt and hose, she lowered herself onto the thickly padded mattress.

He stripped off her hose and gazed at her bare legs and the dragon's tail. He touched her ankles and traced the tattooed tail to her navel.

For the next hour she pleasured him.

Afterward, Leland fell asleep. His Rolex read ten-thirty. She crept out of bed, gathered her things and went to the bathroom. She laid her clothes across the dressing table, did a quick clean-up and put on fresh makeup. It dawned on her that she had added one more day to the best three days of her life.

She dressed and went back to the bed. Leland was still asleep. *I really did good by him*, she thought. She gently shook his shoulder, and stared into his eyes when he opened them.

"Leland, I have to go. I enjoyed our time together and hope to see you soon."

"I'll be flying from New York to L.A. on Wednesday. I can stop by and see you then?"

Marti gazed around the room. Leland liked the best in everything—hotel suites, top brand liquor, imported Italian suits, and custom-made leather shoes. DeMarcus had warned her, *Don't make dates when they don't even know if they going to be in town*. Time was money and she couldn't be waiting around for some CEO or CFO or whatever was Leland's title. "Why don't you call the agency Wednesday when you leave New York?"

"I've got something for you." He reached for his slacks, removed his billfold and pulled out five Benjamins. She grabbed them, a $500 tip, and stuffed the bills in her handbag. Then she gently wrapped her fingers around his neck and parted his lips with her tongue.

"Thank you so much, sweetheart," she whispered in his ear.

He caressed her breast.

Marti realized she had a cash cow here. But it was time for her to go. She was getting money to start her secret fund, to replace the money stolen from her. The secret "get clean" fund that DeMarcus wouldn't know about. The fund that would bring her and Tanya together again. She gave Leland one more look and blew him a kiss.

He sank back against the pillow, and after a minute Marti heard Leland snoring. She tiptoed to the door, opened it, snuck into the hallway and closed the door behind her. *I hope the next one isn't a wrinkly old fart.*

She checked her appearance in the elevator's mirrored doors for john number two. She licked her finger and tucked a loose strand of hair behind her left ear, then wiped off a lipstick smudge above her lip. She liked what she saw.

She opened her handbag, lifted three of the hundred-dollar bills out, and snapped the bag shut. *Honest, DeMarcus, Mr. Grayson only gave me a two hundred-dollar tip.* She giggled as she stuffed three hundred dollars into her bra. The elevator doors opened and she paraded into the lobby. Her nervousness was gone. Her long legs took her to the front doors in seconds. She felt porters and hotel guests gawking at her and enjoyed every second of it. The doorman opened the door for her and she stepped under the canopy.

The black El Dorado pulled up to the curb. The doorman rushed down and opened the passenger door. Marti stepped up, and the doorman opened his hand to her. She placed her palm in his and stepped into the Cadillac.

DeMarcus laid his hand on the back of her seat and leaned toward her. "Well, how was it?"

"It was good. He was the perfect gentleman. He wants to see me next Wednesday—"

"Tell him—"

"I know. I told him to call the escort service."

"I told you you'd be good." He put the car in gear and pulled away. "Your next client is in a hotel not too far from here."

"Is it as nice as that hotel?"

"Not quite. But the man is younger. He's about fifty."

"That's good, old Leland was wrinkly. But he was nice."

DeMarcus made a right turn, a left at the next corner and stopped in front of a narrow building. A dim light hung over a revolving door.

"This is it?"

"Not everyone can afford a thousand a night. Speaking of money, how much did he tip you?"

Marti opened her purse, wrapped her fingers around a hundred-dollar bill and extended her hand toward DeMarcus.

He leaned forward, grabbed the bill and fell back into his seat. "One hundred bucks? You're bull shitting me."

"He gave me two hundred. You get half, right?"

"Am I gonna have to strip search you?"

She swallowed. "All he gave was two hundred."

He slid across the seat and jammed his hand up her dress.

Marti locked her knees together and pushed his hands away. "What're you doing?"

"Gonna check your garter belt and then your bra. I know you're used to stashing bills in garters." He lunged at her again.

She shoved him in the chest. "You're going to mess me up and the next john is going to bitch to the escort service."

He sat back. "Don't be too smart for your own good. Get up there, 303."

Marti opened the door, stepped out and slammed it shut. She looked up at the neon sign under the third floor windows—*H tel Internationale*. The letter *o* was burned out. There was no doorman, just a revolving door with smudges on the glass. She stepped up to the door and pushed the handle. It felt sticky and she pulled her hand away. She turned, looking for DeMarcus, but the El Do was gone. She braced her handbag against the handle, shoved it and entered the lobby.

This place was nothing like the previous hotel. In a cubbyhole to her left was a counter. Seated on a stool behind the counter was a bald man, eyes closed, elbow on the countertop, chin resting in his palm. A soft rumble from him told her he was asleep.

Marti walked past the sleeping clerk to a small elevator. The door wasn't much wider than her shoulders. She hit the button and it creaked open. The carpet inside was worn and smelled moldy, the tin walls engraved with vulgar expressions. The door closed. She tapped the button marked three and the elevator jerked up. After several jerks it came to a shuddering stop and the door opened. *This is worse than the Pole Club*, she thought.

She crept down the hallway, where antique-looking wall sconces cast their dim beams down wallpaper from a past era. She reached the door marked 303 and heard classical music coming from the room. She knocked. The music stopped and she knocked again. The sound of boots marching across the floor grew louder.

"*Da*," a man said from inside.

"This is Mercedes. I'm from the escort service." she whispered through the thick wood.

"*Da*." The door opened. "*Dobryj vecher.*"

She saw a fat bald man, four inches shorter than her, wearing a baggy beige suit.

"You speak English?" she asked.

His head tilted from side to side and he waved his hands, palms up. "Little."

"Did you call for a date?"

"*Da*, yes." He smiled, took her hand and yanked her into the room, then locked the door and turned to face her. He thrust his left hand toward her, pulled his sleeve up and pointed to his Timex. "Blow job, fast."

Marti started a slow dance, moving her hips from side to side. She turned her back to him, reached around and slipped her zipper down, and stepped out of her dress.

He marched over to a club chair, sat down and lifted a bottle of Stolichnaya off the end table, screwed the cap off and poured a few ounces into a glass. He tightened the cap back on the vodka, set the bottle on the end table and emptied the glass. He licked his lips as he watched Marti dancing, pulled his left sleeve up and again pointed at his watch. "Blow job, fast, meet comrades soon."

He pulled his zipper down, spread his legs and grabbed Marti's hand, pulling her onto her knees between his legs. She could smell his sweaty flesh.

"I know you," he said.

Marti shook her head. "I don't think so. I'd remember you."

"We not meet, but I see you."

"Can't be," she said.

"Yes, I remember dragon on your back. I see you at my brother Drazen's Pole Club, yes?"

Marti froze, thought *holy fuck* and then shot upright. "No, no." She grabbed the bottle of vodka and smashed it against the man's skull.

He shook his head, looked up with glazed eyes and reached for the bottle.

She swung it again, striking his left temple. He fell against the armrest. She pounded the bottle against his head again and again. He fell to the floor, blood gushing onto the carpet.

Marti's chest rose and fell with each rapid breath. "Oh, my God."

She put the bottle on the end table and dropped to her hands and knees, lowering her ear to his nose and mouth. She didn't hear any breathing. She swayed back onto her haunches and went through his pockets, found a wallet and lifted a business card out of it. She dropped the wallet, held the card up and read it.

Petrov Ivanov

Consular Division of the Embassy of the Russian Federation

2641 Tunlaw Road, N.W.

Washington, D.C.

202-555-8913

"Shit, Ivanov." Marti stood, slipped the card in her bag, and quickly dressed. She hurried to the door, then stopped, went back to the body and picked up the wallet. It was full of hundreds and fifties. She grabbed a handful and stuffed the wallet and cash in her handbag. She stepped over Petrov's body and hurried to the bathroom, grabbed a towel and returned to the end table. "Drazen's brother, Marko's uncle, here's a couple for those fuckers." She wrapped the towel around the bottle of Stoli and swung it twice more, cracking Petrov's skull where it still looked intact. "Once for each asshole." Then she placed the bottle back on the end table, wiped it off and left the hotel.

Chapter 17

Saturday, midnight

THE CALL FROM DRAZEN CAME over Marko's cell. "We've got to find Marti and the twenty thousand dollars," Drazen said. "The longer we wait, the more difficult it will be. You and Luka come to my office now."

Marko left his post at the front door of the club, with Luka trailing him. They pushed through the crowd of drunken customers and the maze of lights, and a few minutes later walked into Drazen's office. Posters of the dancers covered the walls. Drazen rolled the tip of his cigar in a glass ashtray, knocking off the ash. "She doesn't know her away around, has no papers, no way to get an airline ticket. Got to be in the fuckin' city."

Luka sat down in one of the metal armchairs in front of Drazen's desk. "We checked the other strip joints. They ain't seen her."

"She's no fool. She knows we would find her if she did that," Drazen said.

Marko leaned against the wall. "Someone must have driven her away."

Drazen shook his head. "I'm sure she had no plan that involved someone else. She just fuckin' walked out during all that commotion over Marchese." He exhaled. "Did you check the cabs around here?"

Marko looked at Luka. They both shook their heads.

Drazen leaned forward. "Well, don't you think that might be a good fuckin' idea?"

Marko shifted away from the wall. Luka stood.

Drazen gave Marko a hard look. "Your Uncle Petrov is in town this weekend. He should call me tomorrow. He'll help us find her."

Luka's eyes narrowed. "What can he do that we can't?"

Marko laughed. "Uncle Petrov is KGB. My father moves money for them from Russia to here and back. I'm sure they would repay my father for his patriotic acts."

"You talk too much, Marko." Drazen waved his hands in the air. "Get off your ass and do something. You check the cabs that come to our door. Luka, go to Edward's Restaurant down the block. They have bands and customers are always coming and going. If you learn anything, I'll tell Petrov."

A little after one a.m. Luka flashed Marti's Pole Club photo to the seventh cabbie that had pulled up to the restaurant. This one was a black man wearing an orange and green Rasta hat. "You see this lady the last few days?"

The man's eyes narrowed. "What you want to know for, mon?"

"Look asshole, if you've seen her, tell me."

"Maybe I have, maybe I haven't."

Luka opened the rear door and stepped into the cab. He pulled a Glock 19 out of his waistband and pushed the barrel against the Plexiglas shield. "A bullet from this pistol will go right through this glass, that mess of hair in your hat and into that little fuckin' pea brain of yours. Have you seen this bitch?"

"You think you're the first mon to pull a pistol on a cabbie? You ain't gonna shoot me right here in front of this place, people all about. I pull up to the door now, you get out and I get the next fare."

Luka stuffed the pistol back in his pants. "Just tell me, have you seen her?"

"How much it worth to you?" The cabbie slid open the fare tray.

Luka reached into his pocket, grabbed a roll of bills, pulled out a fifty and put it in the tray.

The driver pulled the tray in and fished out the fifty. "She paid me a lot more than this."

"Mother fucker." Luka shook his head. "How much?"

The cabbie got a crafty look. "Let's see how much Jamal remembers. First she gives me five twenties and then a hundred. No, wait, a hundred and five fifties. No, no, I was right, five twenties and then we stop at ATMs and she gives me two hundreds. Or was it—"

"Enough, I'll give you two hundred now. You take me everywhere you took her and I'll give you another two hundred when we're done."

"I can do that." He pushed the tray open. "One hundred fifty more now, please."

"Fucking thief." Luka took a hundred and a fifty from his roll and stashed the bills in the tray. "Before you take me to where you took her, stop at the Pole Club. We have to pick up one more guy."

"Okay, mon. Second passenger, another fifty dollars." He pulled away from the curb and headed to the club as Luka dropped another fifty into the open tray.

At the Pole Club, Marko joined Luka in the back seat of the cab. Ten minutes later, the cabbie turned into the drive-thru at First National Bank.

"What the fuck are you doing?" Marko said.

"Your friend tell Jamal to go everywhere he take the lady. This first stop."

"What the hell did she do here?" Luka asked.

"She go to cash machine and come back mad."

Marko moved to the edge of the seat and leaned against the divider. "What do you mean? She didn't have any bank accounts."

"She come back with no money. Then she look in little book and find secret numbers, so she goes back to cash machine and comes back with lots of money. She gives some to me because I told her she needed secret numbers."

Marko looked at Luka. "Had to be Marchese's bank accounts." He turned and banged on the Plexiglass. "Okay let's get out of here. Where did you take her next?"

"To another bank, and then another one and then one more."

"That bitch, she's rolling in dough," Luka said.

"Do you remember the names of the banks?" Marko asked.

"I don't remember names but I remember places. I can drive you to them."

"Let's do that fast and then you take us anywhere else you took her," Marko said.

"Fast is an extra fifty dollars." The fare tray slid back to the passenger side.

"Jesus Christ." Marko pulled a fifty out of his pocket and stuffed it in the tray.

Jamal drove the cab to the next three banks he had taken Marti to, and Luka wrote down their names on a fare envelope the cabbie sold him for ten dollars.

"Where did you take her next?" Marko asked.

"She get sick and I take her to gas station. She go to the bathroom."

"Was there an ATM at the station?" Luka said.

"I don't know."

"Take us there," Luka said.

Marko shook his head. "We don't need to go there."

Luka's eyes narrowed and he folded his arms across his chest.

"Where next, Jamal?" Marko said.

"She need some smack to get better, so I take her to the West Side."

"Let's go." Marko settled his Glock deep in his waistband.

Twenty minutes later they were heading north on Kildare from Madison. Jamal pulled to the curb and put the cab in park. "I drop you off at 206 building, where she went. Go to apartment 2B and tell man at the door Patchie sent you."

Luka and Marko got out of the cab. As Jamal shifted into gear, Marko stuck the barrel of his Glock through the open window, against the back of the cabbie's neck. "Jamal's not going to leave us here. He's coming with us, and he's not getting any more money."

Jamal froze. "You can't shoot me here. People will see."

"Here anyone can get shot and no one will see." Marko opened Jamal's door and yanked him out by his collar.

Jamal stumbled and fell onto his hands and knees. Marko pulled him up while Luka took the keys out of the cab's ignition.

Shouts of *five-oh* echoed across the courtyard. They heard shoes scuffing on hard clay and doors creaking as silhouettes disappeared into the night.

"Lead the way, Jamal." Marko shoved him toward the door of the building.

The cabbie looked over his shoulder. "You should pay Jamal for this."

"Shut up and take us to 2B."

Jamal marched ahead, followed by Marko with his Glock at his side, and then Luka. In front of the building, Jamal waved his arms palms up. "Drop lady off here but I don't know if she went in."

Marko shoved him against the door. The naked light bulb above it was just bright enough to make six bullet holes visible. Marko racked the slide of his Glock back and chambered a round. "Don't worry, Jamal, I've still got fourteen in the magazine.

"Please don't shoot." Jamal sounded shaky now.

Luka lifted his Makarov 9mm semi-auto from his waistband.

"Oh, shit," Jamal said, and pushed the door open.

They crept up the stairs, Jamal in the lead. They turned on the landing between the floors. Jamal hesitated. The Fugees's *Fu-Gee-La* was beating down from the second floor.

"Go, Jamal," Marko whispered, and shoved him. Jamal tripped on the first stair and stumbled hard onto the staircase. The music stopped.

Marko ran past Jamal. Luka followed. Marko banged on the door to 2B.

"What the fuck you want?" a voice yelled.

"Looking for Marti. She was here last Tuesday," Marko said.

"We don't have no names here."

"Open the fucking door."

"Fuck you. Get outta here."

"Open the door or I'll kick it in."

"Get the fuck outta here."

Marko leaned back, then thrust all his weight forward and kicked the door just to the left of the doorknob. The cheap wood vibrated, held, but the frame loosened. He kicked it again. Two bullets ripped through the door from the other side. The blasts seared their eardrums. Wood splintered into the hallway. The projectiles whizzed past Marko's head. Four more shots screamed through the door. Marko fell backward into Luka and they tumbled down the stairs.

"Marko, are you all right?" Luka asked. He pushed Marko off and felt something damp and spongy clinging to his neck and dripping down his shirt.

Luka shoved Marko to one side. He crumpled to the floor. Luka stood over him. Marko's right eye was gone. Blood gushed from two wounds in his chest and another in his abdomen.

"Jamal, help me," Luka said.

There was no answer.

Luka gazed down the stairs. Jamal was gone.

Chapter 18

Sunday, 2:30 AM

Special agent William Richmond and homicide detective Steve Hamilton flashed their badges at the officers acting as doormen at the entrance to the Pole Club and walked in. The music blasted away and lights danced over the naked girls gyrating around the brass poles. The bouncer at the interior door approached them.

"Is Drazen Ivanov here?" Richmond asked.

"Not sure. Why you want to know?" The bouncer gave them a bemused look, as if he thought them an unlikely pair. Richmond was African-American, a shade under six feet with hair starting to gray at the temples. Hamilton—white, broad-shouldered and bald—towered over the bouncer. His face had a permanent grimace that made people want to talk about whatever he wanted to know. Richmond figured that was an asset.

"We're the police. It's about his brother," Hamilton said.

"I'll call him." The bouncer spoke into a microphone protruding from his sleeve, lifted his hand over the earpiece he wore and then said, "Go to the door with the *Private* sign over it. He'll meet you there." He pointed to the left of the bar.

Richmond and Hamilton walked over. Customers turned their heads as the men passed by, probably wondering what punishment the big guy was going to dispense and to whom.

Inside his private office, Drazen Ivanov sat behind his massive wooden desk and watched as his two visitors flipped open their identification. He gave each man's badge close scrutiny, then laced his fingers together behind his head and leaned back in his chair. "Sit down, gentlemen. This must be important, perhaps an international incident of some kind to bring the FBI and Chicago police out in the wee hours of the morning. Or tell me, should I call an attorney before I say anything else?"

Both men remained standing. "Do you have a brother by the name of Petrov Ivanov?" the one named Hamilton asked.

"Yes. Is he in trouble?"

"I regret to inform you he was murdered sometime late yesterday night or early this morning. Sorry for your loss," Hamilton said.

Drazen shot forward in his chair and slammed his hand on his desk. "Are you sure? There's no mistake?"

Hamilton took an envelope out of his suit coat. "I have a photo, but I should warn you, he was badly beaten. I can show you the photo for temporary identification if you'd like."

Drazen nodded. Hamilton opened the envelope, took out the photo and slid it across the desk.

Drazen picked it up, examined it and closed his eyes. He bowed his head and then looked up at Hamilton and Richmond. "Do you know who did this? Did you arrest anyone? My poor Petrov."

Hamilton shook his head. "No one has been arrested yet. It looks like it might have been a robbery. His wallet is missing. We found identification in his briefcase and your business card. That's what led us to you."

Drazen blinked away the watery burn in his eyes. "Why is the FBI involved?"

"We were notified because Petrov was an employee of the Russian government. I've sent a wire to the State Department. They'll notify the Russian embassy when it opens," Richmond said.

"He was going to meet me for supper tomorrow." Drazen shook his head. "My younger brother, my only one."

His cell phone rang. He looked at it, shut it off and shoved it in his pants pocket.

"It could be a robbery, but the way he was beaten looked typical of a heated argument, like whoever attacked him was enraged. Do you know of anyone who'd be angry with him, or any enemies he had?" Hamilton asked.

"No. As far as I know, he was just coming to visit me and my family."

"Why was he staying in the Gold Coast area? You don't live near there, do you?"

A light on Drazen's desk telephone blinked. He pushed the phone to the far corner. "I live in Winnetka. He often stayed on the North Side when he visited, liked to go to the bars and fancy restaurants."

Three knocks came at the office door. Drazen gave it a dismissive wave, as if the person on the other side could see. "I'm busy, go away."

Another knock. "Didn't your hear me? Go the fuck away," Drazen snapped.

"Mr. Ivanov, Luka's on the house phone. He tried to call you on your cell. He said it's urgent."

"What could be so damn important? All right, I'll take it." He pushed the blinking light on the desk phone and put the receiver to his ear.

As he listened, his head buzzed hot with anger. "What?" He felt like someone was twisting a knife in his gut. Electric pain screamed in his mind, though he made no sound after his first shocked exclamation.

Finally he put the receiver down, raised his head and looked at the two men standing in front of him. His temple pulsed and he felt tremors in the patch of skin under his right eye. "My son was killed. Shot to death."

Chapter 19

Sunday, 2:30 PM

SCOTT SAT NEXT TO BILLY ON the sofa in the living room. "I'm going to Father Dugan's church. I'll be back around four forty-five. Will you be all right?"

Billy's forehead wrinkled and he looked into his father's eyes. "You didn't go to Mass this morning, why are you going now?"

"It's about those pills Father Dugan took with him. I've gotten…stuck on them and I need help so I can stop taking them. I don't need them for the pain anymore."

"How's he going to help you?"

"He's not helping me directly. There's a group of people who're stuck on pills and other stuff, and they support each other trying to change the way they deal with things they're stuck on. It's like being sick and helping each other get better."

"Sure, Dad, you know I want you to get better." Billy gave Scott a hug.

"Me too, Billy. So I can be a good father for you. I'll have my cell phone, so if you need anything, call me. Don't wait because I'm in the meeting. Okay?"

"Yeah. Have a good meeting."

Scott arrived for the Narcotics Anonymous meeting a few minutes before three. He felt clammy, perspiration dripping down his torso, and his stomach roiled. He wondered if it was just nervousness about confessing his addiction to a group of strangers, or symptoms of withdrawal.

As before, thirteen chairs were scattered around the circular table in the upstairs room. On a smaller table against the wall, a coffee urn dripped into a twelve-cup pot. A second pot was already filled. Three stacks of Styrofoam cups, a carton of powdered creamer, a box of sugar and another of plastic spoons sat next to packages of chocolate chip cookies. Next to the cookies was a stack of Narcotics Anonymous handbooks.

Scott nodded at Jorge, who was by the coffee urn. When Scott went over to get himself a cup, they shook hands.

"Glad to see you came back," Jorge said. He took two cups and filled them with coffee. "I assume you'd like some."

"Thanks, I'll take mine black." Scott watched as several more people came into the room. Many of the faces looked familiar, even though he hadn't thought he'd paid too much attention last week. Sitting in the far corner was a man with gray hair and horn-rim glasses. *I know that guy from somewhere*, Scott thought.

Jorge took a sip of his coffee. "We better get more chairs. Sometimes it's standing room only and my back can't take that for an hour and a half."

They went and fetched three more chairs and set them up. Within the next few minutes the room filled, until all but two chairs were taken. Jorge called the meeting to order. "Welcome, old friends and new friends.

If you don't have a booklet, please take one off the side table and we'll get started."

This time, Scott listened as things progressed. Jorge took the group through their statement of purpose and general announcements, and then started open sharing. Several people raised their hands, announced their first names and that they were addicts, and talked about their successes and failures. After each person finished speaking, the group applauded and thanked him or her.

Scott glanced at his watch. Four-fifteen. The meeting would end soon. He swallowed and raised his hand. A cold current of dread ran down to his intestines as Jorge nodded at him.

"Go ahead, Scott," Jorge said.

He felt them all staring at him, and glanced at the floor. "I'm Scott and I'm a nar—" He cleared his throat. "A narcotics addict." It was the first time he'd ever said that. He pushed his hand through his brown hair and looked up, able to watch the others' faces now as he told his story. "I used to be a federal agent. I got shot by a corrupt agent during the execution of a search warrant."

He shifted in his chair. "In the hospital I kept hallucinating, reliving the experience again and again. I could smell the stench of the public bathroom where it happened, and I thought I was going to die without seeing my son one more time. My wife left me and took our boy with her. I felt someone holding my hand. Thought it was an angel. I opened my eyes and it was my boy."

He paused. His eyes welled and he wiped away the tears with his forefinger. "But that's another story. Anyway, a bullet was lodged too close to my spine to be surgically removed and I became addicted to painkillers. After eight months of physical rehab I was put on disability because the bureaucrats thought I was too great of a liability. The painkillers have become a way of life for me." He kept the one secret he couldn't yet reveal—that his father committed suicide because the old man had abused him, and that Scott had received therapy because he might be a threat to his own son. "That's all I have to say now."

His new friends applauded and thanked him, without any judgment. Scott nodded. He felt as if a weight had been lifted from his chest.

Jorge closed the meeting with a reading of *Just For Today*, and together they read the Serenity Prayer from the booklet. Everyone rose, the sound of chairs scraping the scarred wooden floor filling the room. They gathered in groups of three and four, sipped coffee and ate cookies. Scott saw the man with the gray hair and horn-rim glasses walking his way.

"Remember me?" the man said. "I was on the task force nine years ago."

"Yeah, I recognize you. You were with the IRS. I don't remember your name. I came on just about the time you were leaving."

"Joe Haller. I was a special agent, retired seven years ago. I heard about your situation, getting shot, I mean. Sorry about that."

"Retired, that's the good life."

"Not really retired. I've got my own forensic accounting practice. Mostly defense work and civil cases, background stuff, due diligence. Got time for a cup of coffee? You can fill me in on what happened with some of the old guys."

"Sure, there's a coffee shop on Madison a block west of Ridgeland. Let me call my kid and I'll meet you there in fifteen minutes."

Scott called Billy and told him he would be about a half hour late, and then went to the coffee shop. Haller was at a booth next to the window overlooking Madison. Two cups of coffee sat on the table.

Scott slid into the booth. "Are you a regular at these meetings?"

"Not here. Actually, my addiction's booze. I've been sober for four years but I still go to meetings a couple of days a week. Got the feeling it was time to drop into a meeting and this was the closest one. Even though it's N.A., not A.A., it still helps. How about you?"

"This was only my second meeting and my first day of sobriety. It's tough. But I know I have to do it. My kid ended up on the West Side a few days ago trying to make few bucks to help me pay the mortgage. I blew everything I had on drugs. I can't let that happen again."

"That should be good motivation. So what're you doing while you're on disability?"

"I just started doing some private investigating. Trying to find a girl that became an exotic dancer and disappeared a few days ago. The last time anyone saw her was at this strip joint, the Pole Club. I followed one of the guys who works there at 4:00 a.m. last Saturday to a low-rent apartment building where they locked the girls up, and then to a mansion in Winnetka."

Haller took a swig of coffee. "Sounds interesting. Who owns the club?"

"Don't know. Trying to figure that out."

"I'm not very busy right now. I've got several software packages that supply corporate data, real estate ownership, vehicles and criminal background. Give me what you have and I can run it through the indices, let you know who you're dealing with."

"That would be great. Thanks, Joe."

Haller opened a leather pouch on the seat next to him, lifted out a yellow legal pad and laid it on the table. "Jot down what you know—license plates, addresses, business names, and I'll run them for you." He handed Scott a business card.

Scott read it. *Joseph Haller. Forensic Accounting, Litigation Support. Riverside, IL 60550, 708-555-1212.* He wrote down the name of the strip joint, the addresses for the apartment building the girls were taken to and the mansion in Winnetka, and pushed the tablet back toward Haller. "Thanks, again. This could be very helpful. I better get home. My boy's waiting."

"I'll call you in a day or two with the results. There's a lot of information available in these packages." Haller reached across the table and Scott shook his hand. He'd heard about these IRS guys, how they could take a stack of documents and make an informative little package out of it. *After all, they got Al Capone*, he thought.

Chapter 20

Sunday, 7:00 PM

THE FORMER GOVERNOR HAD HIS typical Sunday. A nine a.m. tee-off time at the country club with his political friends, a poker game afterwards and then the evening with the wife, Katherine, in their Lake Shore Drive condo with a view of Lake Michigan. He plopped down into his recliner, watched the red and green lights of the remaining boats out on the lake. *I should get Jeanie out there and rock that boat, sink or swim, baby.* The thought made him laugh.

"What's so funny?" Katherine asked. She was a thick-bodied woman, thirty years older than Jeanie.

"Oh, I was, ah…I was thinking of the golf game today. Bet Burl a hundred bucks on the last hole that he wouldn't beat me and he four-putted. It was a sucker bet." He laughed again.

"You shouldn't bet so much. He's an old friend."

Everson unfolded the Sunday newspaper, held one edge in his left hand with the rest spread across his lap. In his right hand was a Macanudo cigar. The tip was a burning ember, the end splayed flat and wet with saliva. Katherine's television program and her endless babble receded into white noise as he devoured world news and local scandals, focusing on any federal foray into state and local politics. *Can't trust that fucking U.S. Attorney,* he thought as he rolled the tip of his cigar in the glass ashtray on the end table next to his recliner. He turned over page three and read the bold print—*Local Man's Son and Brother Killed in Separate Incidents.* The name jumped out at him—*Ivanov.* He was so surprised, he swore out loud. "Holy shit."

"I wish you wouldn't use that kind of language. What would the public say?" Katherine said.

He ignored her. "I don't fucking believe it."

"James."

"I'm going to my office, got to make a call." Everson lodged the cigar between his teeth. Smoke leaked slowly from his mouth as he pushed the button on the remote and the recliner rose to an upright position. He stood and marched down the hall, leaving a trail of newspaper scattered across the hardwood floor.

Everson closed the office door behind him, then went and sat behind a large desk in a black leather chair. He yanked his cell phone off his belt and hit six on the speed dial.

Drazen's voice came over the line. "Yeah?"

"It's the King. I just read the paper. My condolences."

"It's a horrible to thing to lose a son and a brother in one night. But the vodka kills the pain."

"What happened?"

A pause before Drazen answered. "It's my fault. I sent Luka and Marko out looking for Marti. They found the cabbie that picked her up the night she left the club. They had him drive them to all the places he took her. At first it was a couple of banks to make withdrawals from ATMs. Then to a drug house on the West Side. Marko tried to force his way in. He always was impulsive. The people inside shot through the door. They killed him. Luka took off before the police came, left Marko's body there with all the niggers. The cab driver disappeared."

She stole the money that was withdrawn from the ATMs, Everson thought. "My man can help you avenge Marko's murder."

"How can he do that?"

"He's good. Give me the address and apartment number, and he'll go out there and find who murdered your son." *And where the girl went, and get my money back.*

Drazen gave him the information and described the building as Luka had told him. "Tell your man to be careful."

"I will, but don't worry about him, he knows how to handle himself." Everson closed his flip phone. *Even if I don't tell him your son was murdered there.*

Chapter 21

Scott's cell phone vibrated. He pulled it off his belt and saw the 312 area code on his caller ID. He rose from the living room couch with a glance at Billy, "I've got to get this," he said, and headed into the kitchen. "Hello."

"Scott, it's Everson. How's my man?"

I'm not your man, you just pay me, Scott thought. "Good. What's going on?"

"Not much."

"Hope you don't mind me calling you on a Sunday night?"

Scott shrugged. "Nope, open 24/7."

"Any news yet on our girl?"

He leaned against the kitchen sink. *The only thing I've checked on was the strip club you told me to stay away from.* "I've got a few leads, checking with different sources, but nothing solid."

"I've got some news for you and I want you to check this out." Everson gave him the address on Kildare. "It's courtyard building with a red lamp at the sidewalk. She was at apartment 2B late last Tuesday night or early Wednesday morning. You know the neighborhood?"

"Yeah," he said, but couldn't tell Everson he used to cop there. "A lot of drug houses in K-town. If I can ask, how'd you get the lead?"

"I really can't say. It's a sensitive situation. You know how those things can be."

"Sure, been there, done that. I'll head over there tomorrow. Thanks, Gov."

"Sounds good." The phone went silent.

He knows a lot more than he's telling me, but I'll find out, Scott thought as he clipped his cell phone back on his belt.

Everson's secrets were getting to Scott. He felt the edge sharpening that only the pills could soften. He grabbed a glass out of the drying rack, went to the refrigerator, filled it with a handful of ice cubes from the freezer and poured Pepsi from a two-liter bottle, then slammed the fridge door closed. His hand shook so much he could hear the ice rattling against the glass. Perspiration beaded on his forehead. He walked out of the kitchen to the stairway and looked up. The pills he'd bought Friday were still in his nightstand.

His phone vibrated. "What the hell does he want now?" He lifted the phone and looked at the screen. A 708 area code flashed across it. Scott answered. "Yeah?"

"Hi, it's Joe."

"Joe?"

"From the meeting Saturday."

"Oh. What's up?"

"I've done some research on the info you gave me. Are you available tomorrow around noon?"

Scott nodded. "Yeah."

"Good. There's an AA meeting at the church in my neighborhood. Let's meet there and we can go for coffee afterward."

Scott furrowed his brow. "Joe, that would be my third meeting in four days. And I don't have a problem with booze."

"We practice the same principles and I bet you weren't planning on going to an N.A. meeting tomorrow. This will keep up your momentum."

Scott exhaled. "All right."

"Good, you're working it." Joe gave him the name and address of the church. "See you there."

After he hung up, Scott brought the glass to his mouth and took a shaky gulp. He looked at Billy sitting on the couch laughing at *America's Funniest Videos*, and thought, *I've got two days under my belt. Tomorrow will be three with a meeting at noon. I can do this.*

Shortly before noon on Monday, Scott traipsed down the stairs on the side of St. Peter and Paul's church in Riverside. He wore a corduroy sport coat, a powder-blue shirt, jeans and loafers. He opened the door and saw Joe Haller amid what looked like three local housewives and a cluster of four men standing near a coffee urn on a table. Just like the set-up at Father Dugan's. As Scott walked in, one of the men broke away from the group and said, "Shall we get started?"

Everyone found a seat on one of the metal folding chairs. Joe grabbed a chair next to Scott. "Glad you made it."

Scott nodded as the chairman greeted everyone, read the preamble and introduced the speaker, one of the women Joe had been standing next to. She was in her mid-thirties, her blonde hair looked like she'd had it done just for the meeting, and she didn't have a ring on her finger. Scott thought, *she's here looking for a husband.* He tried to listen to her but couldn't. The words he'd said at Saturday's meeting, "My name is Scott and I'm a narcotics addict," rattled through his brain. He didn't know if he had the courage to admit it again, at least not in front of a group of strangers or maybe even to himself.

The lady finished speaking, taking more than her fair share of the time, and Scott was late joining the applause. When it came to his turn to speak, he passed. Not long afterward, the meeting came to a close.

"I usually go for coffee with the group but let's go to my house," Joe said. "I'll put some coffee on, we can talk there. I've got a lot of things to tell you."

It was a short walk from the church to Haller's house, a modest two-story white stucco with a side drive and a two-car garage in the back. They entered through the back door directly into the kitchen. It was clean but not updated. The walls were painted yellow and the cabinets white. Haller went to the sink, poured water into a Mr. Coffee, opened a coffee tin and dropped a couple of scoops into the basket where the grounds went.

"My wife always planned to remodel the place. I kept on putting her off. Told her when I retire. But it never happened. Sit down, it'll be a few minutes." He leaned against the sink and pointed at a round butcher block table between two wicker chairs.

"Your wife home?"

"No, she got sick so I retired early to take care of her. She passed a couple of months later."

"Sorry, Joe. I didn't know."

"The sicker she got, the more I drank, and even more after she was gone. Started getting blackouts, was hospitalized a few times. I finally realized it didn't make any sense living like that. I joined AA, been sober since then. Not that I haven't had my moments. That's when I call my sponsor and lean on him. He's helped me through some tough times. So how're you doing?"

"I'm on day three. I was ready to pop a couple pills last night and then you called. You helped and didn't even know it."

"Hey, that was a pure accident. But you've got my cell, so don't hesitate to call anytime. What say I show you what turned up on that stuff you gave me?" He poured two cups of coffee, set them on the table and took a fat manila folder out of a black leather shoulder bag on the kitchen counter. He set the folder down in front of Scott.

Scott opened it and looked at the stack of paper. "I'm not too good at this paperwork. You better tell me what all this means."

"You all right with black coffee? I've got cream and sugar if you want."

"No, this is good." He took a sip.

Joe sat across from him. "I've got software that can access most county real estate records, municipal courts, state incorporation documents, arrest records, and just about any other public records. The first document shows Drazen Ivanov as the owner of that house in Winnetka. He purchased it 1986 and it's mortgage free."

Scott lowered his cup to the table. "You've got to be kidding. That place is a mansion. Shit, I bought my three-bedroom place a year later and I've still got twenty years to go on my mortgage."

"According to county records, the strip club property is owned by a corporation." Haller skipped through a couple of pages. "The New Russ Corporation. The *Tribune* ran an exposé on slum landlords a few years ago, and guess whose name popped up. Drazen Ivanov. That article listed several apartment buildings on the south and west sides and in a few suburbs that they tied to Ivanov, but they were nominally owned by the Petersburg Real Estate Corporation."

"Any of those apartment buildings located close to the strip club?" Scott asked.

Haller dug out a copy of the newspaper article. "Let's see." He scanned the printout. "Here's three consecutive addresses that can't be more than a mile or two from the club."

"One of those has got to be the apartment building he kept the girls in." He described in detail how he'd followed the van and the black Mercedes from the Pole Club to the apartment building. "I see the lights go on in the third floor apartment, and all the windows have bars on them. Who puts burglar bars on the third floor? It was like a prison. That's probably why the girl ran away."

"The Petersburg Corporation owns one more piece of real estate. A shopping center in Mount Prospect. That's where the corporate offices are located."

Scott shook his head. "This guy's a millionaire."

"You read yesterday's paper?"

"No, why?"

"It's not all good news for Drazen Ivanov. Saturday night his son and brother were killed in separate incidents." Haller pulled out the article he'd snipped out of the paper and gave it to Scott.

Scott read it. "That son of a bitch, Everson, he's the one that hired me to find the girl. He called me last night and told me he got a lead from a contact that the girl was last seen at this same address where Ivanov's son was killed. Didn't mention a thing about the son being shot."

"Everson. Wait a minute." Haller shuffled through the documents. "Here it is. A lawyer by the name of Bert Abrams is the registered agent for the New Russ and Petersburg corporations. Guess where he works? Everson and Associates."

"God damn. Everson is the Russian's attorney. He's been stringing me along from day one. Joe, you licensed to carry a concealed weapon?"

"As a matter of fact I am. Got a Glock 20."

"How about you accompany me to that address in K-town and we find out what the hell is going on?"

Haller laughed. "Sure enough, if you can afford my rates."

Chapter 22

FBI Chicago Office
Monday, 2:00 PM

SPECIAL AGENT RED O'MALLEY WAS assigned to the Eastern European Organized Crime Squad. He was fifteen years into his career but only a few pounds over his playing weight from his days on the Boston College hockey team. A clerk dropped off an indices check of the names reflected in the latest transcript of a wiretap he had obtained on the telephone from the office at the Pole Club. He looked at the summary of names mentioned in the transcript. *Ivanov, I know all about you and your kid Marko; Luka Last Name Unknown, get that sooner or later; Marchese, some mafia wannabe looking for some action.*

The summary listed the page numbers where each individual participated or was mentioned in a monitored conversation. He flipped through the pages. "Let's see what the Russkies had to say about Marchese."

Marko Ivanov: "Yes."

Drazen Ivanov: "You find Marti?"

Marko Ivanov: "No, she's not in the van."

Drazen Ivanov: "Shit. Marchese told Luka he had a package for me but I find nothing and his wallet's missing. Bitch must've taken it. She can't have gone too far. I got the bouncers checking the streets. We can't let her get away. Talk to the girls. One of them must know the bitch's plan."

Marko Ivanov: "Okay, Papa."

O'Malley closed the file. *Sounds like the Italians are supplying the Russians with some dope.* He checked the summary page and found the next entry for a conversation mentioning Marti.

Drazen Ivanov: "We've got to find Marti and the $20,000. The longer we wait the more difficult it will be. You and Luka come to my office now."

O'Malley raised his eyes to the ceiling. *Or the dago was bringing money to pay the Russians for dope.* Who had open cases on Marchese? He thought a moment, then made a copy of the pages with the conversations and headed to the other side of the office. Red walked with a slight limp, almost undetectable, from his days on the hockey team.

He stopped in front of Agent William Richmond's desk and tossed the pages from the manuscript of the wiretap onto it. "You owe me a drink."

"Last time I owed you a drink it turned out to be more like a half dozen."

O'Malley put his hands on his hips. "Hey, I'm an Irishman. What do you expect? Besides I'm about to save one of your cases from dying."

Richmond laughed. "It's more like you'll get me transferred to Bismarck, North Dakota."

"Read it, you'll see." O'Malley brushed his hand through his red hair.

Richmond read the two pages and chuckled. "You don't have to be concerned about me killing this case. One of the dancers at the Pole Club killed him."

"You're shitting me."

Richmond glanced at the date on the transcript. "We had a surveillance on Marchese that night. Unfortunately, we ended it seeing him carried out in a body bag. Too bad, because between us and the tax guys we were getting ready to indict the puke. The guy was throwing hundred-dollar bills down all over the city. He had a couple of Corvettes and a quarter-million dollar boat in Boca. Everything paid for in cash."

"What about this girl, Marti? Sounds like the Russians put an APB out on her and twenty grand she took off of him."

"I never heard of her. She's probably the one that did him in and took the twenty G's. He handles a lot of city contracts, could have been from payoffs."

O'Malley pulled the chair out from in front of Richmond's desk and sat down. "This Russian, Drazen Ivanov, is loaded. The last three years he's deposited ten mil into his accounts from all over the world—Switzerland, Cyprus, Germany, Russia plus a couple of hundred thousand in cash. He only paid out about eight million. We think he's laundering money for somebody and the two mil he kept is his commission. We just don't know who yet."

Richmond thumped his fingers on his desk. "Maybe we need to find this girl before the Russians do. She might know something."

"I don't think your boss wants you working a case on a dead puke."

"Remember Watergate, follow the money. It could lead us to something good."

Red scratched his head, "Where do we look?"

"We know she's not at the strip club. Maybe we should try the last place Marko went." Richmond took a newspaper out of his briefcase, unfolded the paper and handed Red the newspaper article covering Marko's murder.

"K-town, what the hell were they doing there?" O'Malley asked.

Chapter 23

Monday, 2:00 PM

An unusual funeral procession, two hearses followed by two black stretch limousines, marked this ordinary Indian summer day. The procession wove its way from Chicago onto the Stevenson Expressway stopping in a rural area near Joliet, in front of two tall red-brick columns with embedded white crosses. Between the columns was a black wrought-iron gate that protected the Russian Cemetery from intruders. A parade of pallbearers dressed in black suits, six on each coffin, half of them armed with semiautomatic pistols tucked in their waistbands, carried the wooden boxes from the hearses past monuments topped by three-barred crosses. The top bar was shorter than the one below it and the bottom bar was at an angle to the others. They stopped at the gravesites and placed the caskets onto the apparatus that lowers them into the grave.

The men were followed by a Russian Orthodox priest and Drazen Ivanov. The priest was dressed in black, a cylinder-shaped hat, a robe down to his shoes, and a long gold chain around his neck with a cross hanging from it. Ivanov wore a black suit and shoes with an open collar white shirt.

Drazen and the priest stood before two graves marked by headstones topped by the three barred cross. The headstones were engraved with the names *Marko Ivanov* and *Petrov Ivanov*. In-between the two excavated gravesites was a patch of grass reserved for Drazen. The twelve pallbearers surrounded the two gravesites. Some of them were bouncers from the Pole Club and others employees from the funeral parlor. They bowed their heads as the priest opened his prayer book.

"O God of spirit and all flesh give rest to the souls of your departed servants. Pardon any transgression which they have committed or thought. Command us to love our enemies and those who defame or injure us and to pray for them and forgiveness. Grant our enemies true peace and forgiveness of sins and help us repay evil with goodness. Amen." The priest closed his book and stepped back.

Cemetery employees slowly lowered the caskets into the ground. Drazen thought, *I'll repay this evil with greater evil.*

Scott drove his Cutlass and Joe Haller rode in the shotgun seat. They stopped at Scott's house, where he ran inside to his bedroom. He opened the closet door, inserted the key into the gun safe bolted onto the shelf, reached in and removed his semiautomatic Sig Sauer 228. It was the same type weapon as the government-issue he'd turned in when he was placed on disability. Scott pulled the slide back and released it. A round jumped out of the chamber. He removed the magazine, topped it off with the round that had been ejected and slapped the magazine back into the pistol. He took the clip-on holster off the shelf, put the pistol in it, and shoved the holster inside his waistband. It was the first time he'd worn a weapon since the wee hours of the morning eight months ago when he was nearly killed. *There's a round in the chamber and I'll never get caught again with my pistol in its holster.*

He returned to the car and they headed to K-town.

"You've had a long layoff. How's it feel doing something like this again?" Haller asked.

"Old habits die hard."

"But the last time wasn't good," Haller said.

"Sometimes when you've done something so many times you get complacent. That won't happen again."

"I've heard your story, Scott. Is there more to it?"

Scott's fingers tightened on the steering wheel. He took a deep breath and exhaled. "My father was a cop. A good one I thought. I was told he was killed in the line of duty. I was a junior at DePaul when it happened, changed my life. That was when I decided to become a cop."

"That's a good reason."

"Not really, it turned out he was corrupt, was screwing some dope dealer's sister on the west side and committed suicide."

"Shit." Haller shook his head.

"A few days before he ate his gun he confessed to our family priest that he had abused me. I don't have any memory of that, but I still live with that possibility…and the fear that it's passed on from one father to the next."

"Man, that's lot to live with, but I can't see you doing something like that."

Scott rubbed the back of his neck and changed the subject to one he could deal with. "We're almost there." He turned north on Kildare and continued as they approached the 200 block. "I had copies of Marti's photo made. They're just from the shoulders up and I wrote my name and cell number on the back. They're in my briefcase on the back seat. I'll drive past the building and go around the block once. You size up the situation. Then get a couple of the photos to bring along."

They drove past the building. "There's one kid leaning against the lamppost, another at the front door and a couple of guys hanging around in the courtyard," Haller said, then leaned to the rear, retrieved a couple of photos and handed them to Scott. "She's got a pretty face."

"I'll show you the whole photo later. She's got a tattoo of a dragon on her back and its tail wrapping up her ankle to God knows where." Scott turned west at the corner. "What do you think?"

"The longer we wait the busier it will get. We either do it now or come back tomorrow morning."

"I vote for now."

"What the hell. Let's go."

They rode past the building one more time and parked around the corner. Scott pushed back his corduroy sport coat, slid his Sig Sauer out of its leather, pulled the slide back and ejected a round. "Just want to double check. Make sure I've got one in the chamber." He removed the magazine, pushed the ejected round in the top of it and slammed it back into the pistol. Beads of sweat moistened the collar of his shirt.

"I always keep a round chambered," Haller said.

"I've got a kid at home. Pistol's under lock and key, but an empty chamber is a good safety precaution. The article said the apartment was on the second floor. I'll be contact, you be cover," Scott said.

"Gotcha."

They got out of the car and walked around the corner. The calls of "five-oh," echoed through the courtyard as they passed a vacant lot and neared the building. Everyone knew there was nothing else two white men in this neighborhood could be but cops. But Scott and Haller weren't.

"Howdy, officers," the boy at the lamppost said.

Scott and Haller nodded and strode down the cracked sidewalk past two men sharing a beverage in a paper bag. They approached a teenager standing in front of the entry way door. His arms were crossed in front of his chest, head cocked and a billed cap tilted at an angle on his head.

"What's up, ossifers?"

"Move over, we've got an appointment," Scott said.

"Wit' who?"

"None of your business. You better move over unless you want to go downtown." Scott pushed his jacket back and put his hands on his hips. The butt of his pistol caught the boy's attention.

The boy nodded. "Be my guest." He stepped aside.

Scott opened the door and pointed at the bullet holes as they stepped into the foyer. There was a large square hole in the wall that once had been filled with mailboxes. An elderly man, balding with thin gray hair, was sweeping the hallway. He nodded at them as they headed up the creaky stairs.

The first door was marked 2A. "There's no bullet holes in this door, let's try the next apartment," Scott said, and headed to 2B. Bullet holes in the door, dried blood on the floor. "This has got to be it." He pointed to the far side of the door. "You stand over there, I'll take this side."

Haller pulled out his Glock and held it down near his leg.

Scott knocked on the door with his left hand. His right hand gripped his pistol. There was no response.

He knocked louder, banging on the door three times. They heard footsteps shuffling.

"Sounds like several people in there," Haller said.

Fifteen seconds later a voice said, "Yeah," from behind the door.

"We're looking for somebody. Want to show you a picture," Scott said.

"You gotta warrant?"

"We're not the police. Just want to show you a photo. See if you've seen this girl around."

"If you ain't the police, I ain't got to let you in."

"We don't want to come in. Open the door and I'll show you the picture."

"I'm tired, just got home from work."

"What's your name?"

"Joe Smith."

Scott looked at Haller, shook his head and mouthed *bullshit*. "Open the door and look at the picture or I'll come back with the real police. You want me to do that?"

"Hold on a second."

Three dead bolt locks clicked and the door creaked open three inches checked by a chain stretching from the door to the doorframe. "Show me your fuckin' picture."

Scott took the photo out of his inside coat pocket and stuck it through the opening. A black thumb and forefinger grabbed it and disappeared into the apartment.

"Ain't never seen her. Now you better get out of here. You interfering with business."

"I know she was here last week."

"I's telling you I ain't seen the bitch."

"My name and number is on the back of the photo. If somebody can give me a lead to her, there could be a reward."

"How much?"

"Depends."

"Depends on what?"

"On how good the information is."

"Now you bullshittin' me. You mean it depends if she alive or dead."

"So you've seen her. Her family is real worried. They're good people. Not looking to hurt you or your business. When and where did you see her?"

"I ain't seen shit. If you ain't the police you better get outta here before some serious problems start up." The door slammed shut and the three dead bolts clicked. Scott and Haller headed down the stairs.

"Son of a bitch," Scott muttered.

"Good try, Scott," Haller said.

"He's seen her. I know it."

Richmond and O'Malley parked a half-block south of 206 Kildare.

"Look, two white guys," Richmond said. "Get the license plate number off their car and run a twenty-eight. Let's see if they're cops or something else. Either way, I want to talk to them."

"They're headed around the corner. Pull up so I can see their car," O'Malley said.

Richmond headed north, passing the street where the car was parked.

"They're getting into an Olds Cutlass. Doesn't look like an unmarked cop car." He keyed the microphone and radioed the plate number into the base station.

Ten seconds later the base returned his call. "The vehicle is a 1989 Oldsmobile Cutlass registered to a Scott Garity," the dispatcher said, and gave them Garity's address in Oak Park.

"Oak Park, that's not far. Let's follow these boys and have a little chat with them," Richmond said. He turned west at the next street and south on Kostner.

"There's the car. He's stopped at Madison." O'Malley pointed with his jaw.

They followed the Cutlass to Riverside where the passenger exited the car and entered a house.

O'Malley jotted down the address. "This will work out good. Better to question them one at a time."

They followed the driver—presumably Garity—back to his house. Richmond parked the Crown Vic a half-block away. "Let's go talk to the man." They walked up the three stairs onto the porch and Richmond knocked on the door.

Can of Coke in hand, Scott watched the two suits come up the stairs. *I guess I'll find out who was following us.* He waited for the knock on the door and opened it. "Can I help you guys?"

Richmond flipped open his credentials, showing his badge and warrant card. "We're with the FBI. I'm William Richmond and this is Fred O'Malley. You mind if we come in?"

"Not at all." Scott took a step back and the agents walked into the living room. "How can I help you?" The agents sat on the sofa and he sat in an armchair across from it.

The one named O'Malley led things off. "Are you Scott Garity?"

"That's me."

"Have you been in the vicinity of 206 Kildare recently?" Richmond asked.

Scott took a sip from the Coke. *Did they see me copping in the neighborhood? Did they have an informant who snitched on me? Is this about today?* "Why do you want to know?"

"It's our job to ask the questions," Richmond said.

"I think I'm entitled to know why the FBI was following me."

"You think you're a smart guy," O'Malley said.

"Look, I carried a badge like you guys for twelve years. I'm on disability now. So tell me what's going on. Maybe I can help you."

"You were with the FBI?" O'Malley asked.

"No, I was a Chicago cop for a few years and on the federal drug task force until last January, when they put me on disability."

"Why'd they do that?" Richmond asked.

"Got shot last January. A month ago, they decided I was too much of a liability." He knew he probably shouldn't say this, but the words came out anyway. "So be careful, guys, don't take a bullet for the job because the G is not going to stand behind you."

Richmond looked at O'Malley and shrugged. "We're trying to find a girl named Marti. She's a potential witness in a case."

"That's what I was doing at the 206 building. Looking for Marti," Scott said.

"Why're you looking for her?" O'Malley asked.

"Her parents sent her to the States from Europe to go to college. She got mixed up with the wrong crowd and disappeared a few days ago. They want her found."

"So you're a licensed private investigator?"

Scott slid his wallet out of his back pocket and removed his investigator's license. "Here, just got it a few weeks ago." He handed it to Richmond.

"Who was the guy with you?" O"Malley asked.

"Joe Haller, a retired IRS special agent."

Richmond handed Scott's license back to him. "How is it that her parents in Europe retained you?"

"Through their attorney, James Everson."

"What led you to the building on Kildare?" O'Malley asked.

"Everson got a lead." *I can be as coy as you guys*, Scott thought. "He didn't tell me the source."

"Maybe we can help each other," O'Malley said. "You get a lead or you find her, can you let us know?" He handed Scott his business card. "We'll do the same."

"Oh, really? Then tell me, why is the FBI looking for Marti?"

"At this point in time we can't divulge that information," O'Malley said.

Scott laughed. "Typical FBI. What happened to your spirit of cooperation?" He gave them his cell number anyway, though. The two agents stood up and Scott walked them to the door. They shook hands, then left his house and got into the Crown Vic.

Scott stood in the doorway and watched the car pull away from the curb. *I've got a feeling there's more to this than a missing girl.*

In the car, Richmond looked at O'Malley. "Do you think he knows about the twenty grand?"

"I'm not sure. You think Everson knows about the money?"

"Who knows. Maybe that's why he hired Garity. Let's check Garity's background. See if we can verify his story, then figure out how we can use him."

CHAPTER 24

FBI Office, Chicago
4:00 PM

RICHMOND AND O'MALLEY SAT IN the ninth-floor office of Supervisory Special Agent Harold Lewis. Lewis had less time on the job than either of them but had taken the fast track, looking for his next promotion, even though he'd been in the management ranks for only two years.

"So what's the result of the indices check on this guy Garity?" Lewis asked.

Richmond held the file in his hands. "He looks clean as a whistle. A couple of years ago he fell into a bag of shit. Corrupt cops in North Hampton set up a guy in a ghetto drug operation. Their lieutenant was extorting the drug dealer for ten grand a month and one of Garity's fellow agents from the federal drug task force got suckered into the mess. Early on the morning of the takedown, Garity was shot, the lieutenant and the bad agent were killed. After eight months of rehab they put Garity on disability."

O'Malley's SSA, Jack Jorgensen, stepped into Lewis' office and closed the door. "Sorry I'm late, was on the phone with the Director. You know, since this covers both of our squads, we've got to run this up the daisy chain to get approval on any monitoring."

O'Malley looked out the window, down at the early rush-hour traffic on Dearborn Street, and shook his head. "We've got to move on this quickly. If by some chance the Russians find that girl Marti, this could be all over. Most likely all over for her."

Lewis folded his hands and leaned back in his black leather judge's chair. "So what do you guys suggest?"

Richmond rested his elbows on the arms of his chair and leaned forward. "Garity looks like a good guy that's been thrown into a difficult situation. I think we wire him up and send him into the governor's office. Have him tell Everson he's got a lead on the girl through an old snitch of his. And then we see what the Gov does."

"Dealing with an ex-governor is a sensitive situation," Lewis said.

O'Malley looked at Lewis, then out the window briefly, and then back at Lewis. "Like Richmond said, time is of the essence. This opportunity could close on us for any number of reasons. I think we send Garity in and spice it up a little. Have Garity give the Gov the same spiel, but tell him the snitch said the girl had a lot of money on her. That'll wet the Gov's beak, motivate him to say something."

Richmond nodded. "I like that."

Jorgensen, leaning against the wall, shifted his weight from one foot to the other. "One thing, guys. What about Garity? Do you think he'll do it?"

"His background is solid. There's no dirt on him," Richmond said.

Lewis rubbed his chin with his forefinger and thumb. "I don't think—"

"You guys go talk to Garity now," Jorgensen said. "I'll start the paperwork. Feel him out. You know how to play it. Sign out the equipment. If it looks good, have Garity call the Gov tonight to set up a meeting for tomorrow."

Chapter 25

5:15 PM

SCOTT WAS ON HIS KNEES in front of the toilet in the second-floor bath, puking his guts out. Each time he vomited it felt like his stomach was being ripped apart. Sweat ran down his face.

His cell phone was on the sink next to the toilet. It rang and he turned his head toward it. The shrill ring tormented him. He reached for it, knocking it into the basin. It rang again and again. The sound vibrated in his head. With one hand on the toilet he pushed himself up, got to his feet and grabbed the phone. The caller ID showed a 773 area code and a number he didn't recognize. He brought the phone to his ear. "Yeah."

"You's one of the white guys came to 206 Kildare the other day?" The voice on the line was scratchy as if burned for decades by cigarette smoke and whiskey.

"Yeah, that's me. Who're you?" Scott asked.

"I's the janitor."

Scott did his best to focus. "What can I do for you, sir?"

"I found this picture of a girl in the garbage. It had a name and telephone number on the back. That's you, right?"

"Yeah, I gave it to the man in apartment 2B."

"Crack heads and coke hoes."

"You know that guy?"

"Praise God, I don't."

"The girl's family hired me to try to find her. The man in 2B said he never saw her."

"He's a liar."

"Did you see her?"

"Yeah. I don't know when she got here or how long she was here, but I saw her leaving last Wednesday morning. Looked like she was coming down hard, all starry-eyed and leaning against the wall, stumbling down the stairs."

"What's your name, sir?"

"You needs that?"

"I might need to talk to you again."

A pause, long enough for Scott to worry. "Eldon Smithfield," the man said finally. "Been the janitor here going on fifteen years. Seen things change a lot, all for the worse."

"This girl you saw, you sure it was the one in the picture?"

"Swear on my Bible."

"You said you saw her stumbling down the stairs. Did you see where she went?"

"Oh yeah, one step out the door and all them hangers-on were trying to do her. But she was smart, just shoved them out of the way."

"Mr. Smithfield, do you live in the building?"

"I got an apartment next to the boiler room. It's in the back in the basement."

"So if I need to talk to you I can find you there?"

"Just as easy to call me. Just 'cause I live next to the boiler room don't mean I ain't got a phone." He gave Scott his telephone number.

"Thanks for calling me, Mr. Smithfield. That was real kind of you."

"I'm a God-fearing man, just trying to do the right thing."

"Thanks again, I'm sure I'll be calling you," Scott said.

"Don't you want to know who she left with?"

"I thought you said she brushed all those guys away."

"Yeah, she did 'til that pimp came along."

"Pimp? You know his name?"

"Everybody on the West Side know DeMarcus DeWayne. I's known him since he was a little boy. He be driving that El Do around. But he don't live on the West Side no more. I hear he up north somewhere."

"You wouldn't happen to know the license plate number on his El Dorado or any other cars he drives."

"Just that El Do. Another pimp had it before and he kept the same plate, LVRBOY."

"Anything else you can think of that might help me find DeMarcus or the girl?"

"Can't think of nothing else. If I hear anything, I call you."

"Thanks, Mr. Smithfield. I may be able to get you a reward if we find her."

"Don't need no reward. Just doing what's right." The line went dead.

It was five-thirty by time Richmond and O'Malley parked in front of Garity's house. The sun was setting and the street lights flickered on.

"Here goes nothing," O'Malley said. "Lewis won't be able to sleep all night as he envisions his career going up in smoke."

"On the other hand, if this works out he'll want you transferred into his squad."

"Shit, I'd rather be transferred to Bismarck."

They got out of the Crown Vic and marched up the stairs. Richmond knocked on the door.

The deadbolt clicked and it swung open. Framed in it was a twelve-year old boy. Garity's son, Richmond guessed.

"What're you guys selling?" Billy said.

Richmond laughed. "Nothing, son. Is your dad home? We'd like to talk to him."

"I'll check. You guys stay here. I'm not supposed to let strangers in the house." The door closed and the deadbolt shot home.

Scott heard a knock on the bathroom door. "What?"

"Dad, there's some men here to see you," Billy said.

"I'll be right down." Scott flushed the toilet, ran some water in the sink and splashed it on his face.

He came down the stairs and approached the door with his phone pressed against his ear. "Joe, I just got off the phone with the janitor from 206 Kildare." He gave Haller the information Smithfield had given him. "Can you check your computer databases and see what you can find on the pimp?"

"Not a problem."

"Great. This has been the toughest day for me yet. Been sweating, aching, puking, and spent most of the day in bed. You going to the meeting tonight?"

"I wasn't going to, but I can meet you there."

"Thanks, I appreciate your support. Be leaving in a couple of minutes. See you there." He shut off the phone, unlocked the deadbolt, opened the door and eyed the agents with weary patience. "What do you want now?"

"Can we come in and talk?" Richmond asked.

"I've got an appointment. I was just on my way out."

"Give us a few minutes and then you can go," O'Malley said.

Scott exhaled and dragged his sleeve across his forehead, wiping the perspiration away. He shook his head. *I don't need this shit now. I'm hurting.*

He turned, narrowed his eyes and looked at Billy, who was sitting on the couch watching TV. "Billy, go upstairs and watch the rest of that program in your bedroom."

"Can't I wait 'til there's a commercial?"

"Go now. These gentlemen are busy and can't stay long because I have an appointment."

Billy tapped the remote, turning off the TV, and tramped up the stairs.

The two agents came in and sat on the sofa. Scott closed the door and sat in an armchair kitty-corner to them. *I need this N.A. meeting, but I can't let them know.* "So," he said, trying for a casual tone. "It's probably not often that someone gets a visit twice in the same day from the FBI. In fact, most people would consider that a bad day."

"It's a good day for you because we're trying to do the same thing you are, Scott," Richmond said.

"And that is?"

"Find Marti," O'Malley said.

Scott crossed one leg over the opposite knee. "We discussed this earlier. I'm supposed to tell you everything I know, you guys say thank you and walk away."

"Nope, this isn't like that at all. We can work together and greatly increase the odds of finding Marti. We know and you know that the longer it takes to find her, the more likely it'll be that she's dead," Richmond said.

"So explain to me how we can work together. I'm all ears."

"I'm going tell you what we know that I don't think you have any idea of," Richmond said. "When Marti ran away from the Pole Club she had a substantial amount of cash."

"An amount in the five-figure range," O'Malley added.

Scott nodded. "That's interesting. How do you know that and who does the cash belong to?"

"I've been looking into Drazen Ivanov, who owns the Pole Club, and I can't divulge how we know about the cash. Let's just say Ivanov appears to be moving money for a variety of people I haven't identified yet." O'Malley leaned forward. "We think there's a connection between Everson and Ivanov."

Scott leaned back in his chair. "Of course there is."

The agents looked at each other, their eyes narrowing.

Scott continued, "I'm sure you checked on the guy I was riding with this afternoon, Joe Haller. He did a lot of background checks on Ivanov for me over the weekend. I'm surprised you don't know this, or maybe you do and you think it's top secret. An attorney in Everson's firm is the registered agent for the corporations Ivanov does business under for his rental properties and the strip joint."

Richmond glanced at O'Malley, who shrugged. "That's interesting. Are you all right? You look sick."

Scott nodded. "I'm okay, just a touch of the flu. Feel a little achy but it's nothing. So what's your plan on how we work together to find Marti?"

"We want you to make a monitored call to Everson and set up an appointment to meet him tomorrow," Richmond said. "Be vague about what you've got for him. Tell him one of your old confidential informants knows a guy that saw Marti at the drug house the night she left the strip joint. Tell him you're meeting your CI and that guy tonight. Your CI promised he's got something good. You can even tell Everson it might cost a little money to make it sound legit."

Scott frowned. *That cover story sounds like the phone call I just had with that janitor, Smithfield. They tap my phone?* "You're kidding me. You want to use me as a witness against the Russian and the ex-gov? You really don't care about the girl. You just want to make a case to get headlines."

"That's how we'll find the girl," O'Malley said.

"Yeah? Even if you make a case against those two assholes, there's no guarantee you'll find her, and if you do, you'll want to use her as witness. You going to put her in the witness protection program, or let them kill her?"

"You're way ahead of the game," Richmond said.

"I'm not way ahead of the game. I know how you play it. Son of bitch, fuck the girl as long as you get your stat."

Richmond shook his head. "You're way off base. Look, the most important thing is to find Marti. If something else comes out of this, so be it."

"So what am I supposed to tell Everson at this meeting tomorrow?"

"That's when you tell him your CI's friend told you Marti had a large amount of cash on her," Richmond said. "Mentioning money will get his interest."

Scott exhaled and leaned forward. He meant to refuse, but then thought, *this might help me find her.* After a moment, he nodded. "Okay."

O'Malley pulled a roll of Scotch tape, a mini-cassette recorder and a microphone out of his suit coat pocket. "I'm sure you know how this works."

"Let's do this, then." Scott grabbed the recorder and taped the microphone to the mouthpiece of his cell phone. He pulled up the address book on his cell and picked out Everson's number.

"I'll do the honors." Scott turned on the tape player and dictated the preamble. "This is Scott Garity. I've given my consent to agents Richmond and O'Malley to tape the call I'm going to place to James Everson from my cell phone to his." He added the time and date, then made the call.

"Hello," Everson's gruff voice answered.

"Governor, it's Garity."

Everson's tone shifted to a blend of relief and anticipation. "My man, a call from you must mean good news."

"I don't want to say I've got something when I don't, but an interesting possibility came up. I contacted some of my old informants from the West Side and had them check around. One of them called back a few minutes ago. A guy he knows told him he saw a girl at the drug house. With the description this guy gave my CI, it's got to be your girl."

Everson sounded guarded now. "That's interesting, but can he lead us to her?"

Scott nodded, as though Everson could see him. "This guy told my contact he saw her leave with another guy, and he can take us to him." He kept the janitor's name to himself. No point siccing the feds on the man.

"I knew you'd do it," Everson said.

"The thing is, this guy will want some money and I'll need to take care of my CI, too."

"That's no problem. How much?"

Scott eyed the FBI agents. "I can't give you a number. I'll check him out and try to figure if this guy is trying to scam us or if he's for real. But I need to know your limit."

"If this is good, I'll go…say two thousand. I mean, I'm sure her family would pay that."

"All right. If he's got good info, how about if I come to your office tomorrow morning and we can discuss where we go from there? Say ten a.m."

"I knew you were the right man for this job. Scott, you do this and I've got some plans for you. You can make some real money."

He couldn't bring himself to say *thank you*. "If I pay this guy, I'll need more cash."

"No problem. See you tomorrow."

The phone went dead. Scott lowered the cell and the agents smiled.

Chapter 26

The Pole Club
Monday, 6:00 PM

DRAZEN SAT AT HIS DESK, in front of him the half-empty bottle of Stoli he had been working on since his return from the cemetery. He screwed off the cap and poured the clear liquid three fingers deep into a Manhattan glass. He picked it up, brought it to his lips and tilted his head back, shooting the liquor down his throat. He grabbed the Nextel phone on the credenza behind him and keyed the push-to-talk button. "Luka, come to my office."

A few minutes later, Luka knocked and announced himself. The door opened a foot and Luka's broad face peered through the gap.

"Come in, my son," Drazen said. At Luka's look of surprise, he explained. "You're the closest living person to family I have left in my life. Well, besides my wife." Drazen waved his hand. "But that is different. You know what I mean."

Luka nodded and closed the door. "You've been like a father to me ever since I met you and Marko was like my brother."

"Sit down, Luka." Drazen swiveled his chair, grabbed a matching glass off the credenza, spun back around and planted it on his desk with a bang. He filled each glass half full. "To Marko."

They picked up their glasses, clinked them together and downed the vodka. Drazen filled the glasses again. "Tell me, my son. Have you ever drawn blood?"

"You mean, killed someone?" Luka swallowed and shook his head.

"It can be a noble thing."

Luka nodded.

"In the old country there were times when I had no choice. Wrongs were done that had to be righted. But I never felt any guilt because there was joy in the killings."

Luka's fingers surrounded the glass and he stared into it.

"When it's done with purpose, then there can be joy." Drazen gripped his glass in his right hand. His fingertips turned white. He rotated his hand counter-clockwise. The clear liquid swished from one side of the glass to the other.

Luka brought his drink to his lips, downing it in two gulps, and placed the glass on the desk.

"I sent my son to his death looking for a whore and dirty money." Drazen shook his head. "May God forgive me. But I don't care what God will do to me for seeking revenge. If He's a just God, He will understand. You understand that the murders of my son and brother must be avenged?"

Luka swallowed. "Of course."

"Revenge for Marko's death will be easier than Petrov's. You must go back to the drug house and kill everyone there. Whoever is there is guilty and not worthy of living. They're either nigger drug dealers or junkies. None will be missed."

Drazen pushed the glasses and bottle to one side. He slid his chair back, lifted an aluminum suitcase from under his desk and placed it on top. He spun the two numerical dials on it, opened it and turned it around so it faced Luka. "Three Uzi pistols with silencers. You pick the two best men to go with you. I will be your alibi and you will be each other's alibis. We will have your timecards showing that you all punched in today and didn't leave until we closed."

Luka's forehead furrowed. "Today?"

"Tonight. Now is the time. My son is buried and this must be done before the motherfuckers disappear into the jungle. I have two thirty-two round magazines for each pistol." Drazen laughed. "You can bring sidearms with you if you want. But you'll have a hundred ninety-two rounds for the Uzis. You know my gratitude to you and the men you select will be eternal."

Luka pushed the suitcase to the side and leaned forward. "And you know you will never have to question my loyalty. I was there, Papa. Marko's body fell into my arms and it was only because of him that I wasn't killed. I want revenge just like you do." He picked up one of the Uzis, yanked the bolt back, pulled the trigger and pretended he was spraying the wall with bullets.

At two in the morning, Luka and his handpicked comrades, Sergei and Mikhail, stole a van from the neighborhood and headed to K-town. They were dressed in black and wore bullet-proof vests and leather gloves. Luka drove past the 206 building and parked in the alley.

He yanked the bulb out of the car's interior light fixture and turned toward his companions. Sergei sat in the passenger seat, and Mikhail crouched on the floor behind him. "Just like I told you in the club, I'll go first. You follow me. We cut through this vacant lot next to the building, making sure no one sees us. We swing around the building and rush down the courtyard to the door. There'll probably be a punk guarding it. I'll shoot him. No one will hear it because of the silencers and that loud nigger music they play. The door to the building shouldn't be locked. If it is, I'll shoot it open. Okay so far?"

Sergei and Mikhail nodded.

"I'll go up the stairs. The apartment is the second door, number 2B. Sergei, you shoot the lock and Mikhail and I will rush in. We shoot everyone we see. Drazen doesn't care if there is one person or twenty. Whoever is there was probably there the night Marko was killed. Sergei, if one of us encounters fire, you come to our aid. We do this for Drazen's revenge. Any questions?"

Sergei and Mikhail shook their heads.

They jacked the Uzis' bolts, preparing the weapons for fire, and crept out of the van. They stayed low in the vacant lot's overgrown weeds, stopping behind the rusted-out Chevy resting on its wheels.

Luka heard Sergei and Mikhail's rapid breathing. "Be calm. They are not expecting us and we have the firepower to take them."

They moved to the next bit of cover, a discarded refrigerator lying on its side. Each man briefly rested on one knee. "Okay," Luka said. "Last stop before we move to the front door. Ready?"

They nodded again.

With Luka in the lead, they rushed around the north side of the courtyard building. Their boots pounded on the hard clay. There was no one guarding the front door.

Luka pushed the door open and spied a shadow coming down the dark staircase. He opened fire, *rat-ta-ta, rat-ta-ta, rat-ta-ta,* like the sound of someone beating a typewriter's keys. The shadow thudded backwards onto the stairs.

They rushed up the unlit stairwell, ignoring the body, to the door marked 2B. Sergei opened fire. The door collapsed inward, and Luka and Mikhail ran into the apartment. The dining room was empty except for worn, dirty mattresses. The room stank of cordite and urine.

Luka rushed back to the kitchen and rear bedroom. Mikhail ran to the living room and front bedroom.

"No one here," Luka yelled.

"These rooms empty, too," Mikhail called out.

"Shit. Drazen won't be happy. Quick, out the back way before anyone comes," Luka said.

He unlocked the rear door as Sergei and Mikhail met him in the kitchen. They ran onto the rear porch and down the stairs to the van. Sergei slid behind the steering wheel, Luka into the passenger seat and Mikhail into the back. "No telephone calls," Luka said. "Drazen wants no record that we were anyplace tonight besides the club. Head to Columbus Park. Ivan will meet us there."

They left K-town and drove west on Madison, then south on Central and west on Jackson into the park. They approached the first tee at the golf course and doused the headlights. Ivan was parked on the street one hundred feet past the starter's building, in a stolen 1990 Buick LeSabre. The van stopped next to it and Luka rolled down his window. "Follow us onto the fairway, into the wooded area behind the second tee."

The van headed to a spot in the middle of the park sheltered by a C-shaped cove of tall oaks and spruces. They parked, and Sergei and Mikhail got in the rear seat of the Buick. Luka took the suitcase with the Uzis from the van and tossed it into the Buick's trunk. Then he and Ivan lifted out two five-gallon containers of gasoline and a set of flares. They poured the gas in the cab and rear of the van, lit the flares and tossed them inside. With a whoosh and a roar, flames engulfed the vehicle.

Luka and Ivan hustled back to the Buick. Ivan drove to the lagoon on the opposite side of the street from the starter's shack. Luka went to the trunk of the car, took the suitcase out and heaved it twenty feet into the lagoon. He watched it sink and then climbed back into the car. "Let's get out of here."

Ivan drove back to the spot he'd stolen the car from and parked it down the block. All four men walked to Ivan's car and drove back to the club.

Luka wondered, *What do I tell Drazen? The only thing I can. I lie.*

Chapter 27

The Pole Club
Tuesday, 3:30 AM

"I'll meet with Drazen alone," Luka told Sergei and Mikhail after Ivan dropped them off at the rear entrance to the Pole Club. "You two throw away the gloves and change your clothes. Put the vests in the liquor storage room. I'll take care of those later."

"What're you going to tell Drazen?" Sergei asked as Mikhail grabbed the door handle.

"That we did our task and did it well. You must never speak of this to anyone. Drazen might ask you, but it will be a test. Tell him we all worked at the club all night 'til closing. Is that understood?"

Mikhail nodded. Sergei put his arm around Mikhail's shoulders. "Come on, let's go finish our shift."

The three men entered the club. Luka went to the liquor storage room and hid the bulletproof vests behind shelves loaded with Jim Beam and Crown Royal. Then he stepped down the hallway and knocked on Drazen's office door.

"Come in," Drazen said.

Luka stepped inside and closed the door behind him.

Drazen nodded toward the armchair in front of his desk. "I trust all went well?" Drazen said.

Luka sat and looked down at the floor before facing Drazen. He swallowed. His mouth felt dry, and he steeled himself not to show his nervousness. "Yes, Papa. I killed the fucker. He tried to escape from the apartment. I filled his body with lead. He died a painful and miserable death. He lies on the stairs where Marko died. I thought that was an appropriate place to leave him."

"Thank you, my son. And your comrades are all safe?"

"Yes, everyone is fine. You were right—avenging your son's death was a noble deed. I'm happy I could do this for you." He glanced at the floor again.

Chapter 28

Chicago FBI Office
Tuesday, 8:30 AM

SCOTT GOT OFF THE ELEVATOR on the ninth floor of the Dirksen Federal Building and held his hands out in front of him. There was a slight tremor from cutting down on the pain killers. He took a deep breath, exhaled and looked west toward the lobby of the FBI offices. The walls and carpeting were government gray. In his corduroy sport coat, a blue shirt and khaki slacks, he probably stood out.

A cute blonde receptionist, likely not more than twenty, sat behind the bullet-proof glass at the lobby desk. To her right he saw a couple of agents tapping codes into secure door locks and then entering the offices. He walked up to the receptionist. "I'm Scott Garity. I'm here to see agents Richmond and O'Malley."

She nodded and smiled at him. "Please take a seat. I'll call them." She picked up the phone and punched in a number as Scott sat in one of eight chairs along the south wall. On the north wall were photographs of FBI Director Louis Freeh and President Clinton.

A few minutes later, Richmond opened the door in the north wall. "Come on in, Scott."

He walked past Richmond, waited a second as the door closed, followed him down a short hallway and entered a windowless interview room that measured ten by ten. O'Malley was seated at a square table. Three more chairs were grouped around the table. On top of it Scott saw a copy of the *Chicago Tribune*, a Nagra tape recorder about the size of a pack of cigarettes, an elastic wrap with a built-in pocket to hold the recorder, a microphone attachment and a roll of gray duct tape.

O'Malley stood and shook Scott's hand. "You look better than you did yesterday. How're you feelng?"

"Great. I can hardly wait to tape record my first client. Great way to start a new career." Scott sat down and put his hands in his coat pockets. Richmond sat next to him.

O'Malley waved his hands over the recorder. "Obviously, you're familiar with the Nagra recorder, but standard procedure requires us to give you instructions. Once we turn it on, we want to minimize any conversation we have so we don't inadvertently record any of our statements that we wouldn't want to turn over to a defense attorney. The recorder shouldn't be turned off unless you're instructed to do so or one of us turns it off."

Scott nodded. "Done it a thousand times when I was sitting in your chair."

"You see today's paper?" O'Malley asked.

Scott shook his head.

O'Malley slid it out from under the tape recorder, opened it to page three and flipped it over to Scott.

16 YEAR OLD GIRL SHOT

Early this morning, in another act of apparent gang violence, Alicia Simpson was shot and killed while visiting her grandmother at 206 N. Kildare. There were no witnesses to the shooting and no one reported hearing gunshots. Alicia was an honor roll student at Marshall High School. No further information has been released.

"Jesus Christ." Scott thought about Billy roaming those same streets trying to pick up fifty dollars to help him pay the mortgage. He exhaled and shook his head again.

"The neighborhood must really be tense," Richmond said. "First Marko Ivanov gets shot, and a few days later a young girl."

"It's really sad that people have to live around that kind of violence," O'Malley said. "Okay. Like we discussed yesterday, we want you tell Everson about your meeting with your make-believe informant last night and his buddy who knows about Marti. Tell him the buddy saw Marti at the 206 building. She bought some dope there and that's when he saw her pull out a roll of cash."

"What kind of dope did she buy and how much?" Scott asked.

"You were the drug agent. What would you say?" Richmond asked.

Scott gave it a moment's thought. "We've got a girl on the run. She doesn't know when she'll be able to cop again. So she'd be buying more than a dime bag, but not so much that she needs something to carry it in. I'd say somewhere between five and ten dime bags. My guess is heroin. It's a more effective drug if you're trying to control someone. That's probably what they're doing at the strip joint, using smack to put the girls down at night. You said she had five figures' worth of cash. Are you talking ten thousand or ninety thousand? That would make a big difference in what she would carry the cash in."

"She had twenty grand, most likely in large bills," O'Malley said.

Scott lifted his hands out of his pockets. "That would be about this thick." He held his forefinger and thumb an inch apart. "I did a lot of one-kilo coke buys and that was usually around twenty grand."

"Okay, so if she folded it in half she could fit it in her pocket. When she ran from the strip joint, I don't think she had time to pack a suitcase."

Richmond glanced at his watch. "It's a little after nine. Let's put the Nagra on and make sure everything is working."

Scott stood, removed his sport coat and shirt and laid them over the back of his chair. O'Malley stretched the elastic band tightly around Scott's T-shirt and fastened the Velcro ends over his stomach. He slipped the tape recorder into the built-in pocket near the small of Scott's back. "How's that feel?"

"I can almost breathe." Scott pulled the Velcro edges apart, let the elastic loosen and attached them again.

O'Malley plugged the microphone feed into the tape recorder and swung the wire over Scott's shoulder, then ripped off a piece of duct tape and secured the microphone near the center of his chest. "We normally use a transmitter on cooperating individuals in addition to the Nagra, but because you're not going into a potentially dangerous situation and you're a former federal agent, we feel you can be trusted. I'm going to turn the Nagra on, so let's be careful with any conversation from this point on."

O'Malley flipped the switch, about the size of the tip of a pen, on the top of the tape recorder. "This is Special Agent O'Malley. I've just activated a Nagra tape recorder on cooperating individual Scott Garity. Did I have your consent to do so, Mr. Garity?"

"Yes." Scott put his shirt and sport coat back on and turned to face O'Malley.

The agent dictated the date and time into the microphone. "We'll walk you out of the building. From there, you're on your own. The ex-governor's office is only a few blocks away on LaSalle. You know the way. If you happen to run into someone you know, just tell them you're late for an appointment and you can't talk now."

"All set?" Richmond asked.

"Let's do it," Scott said.

They walked into the lobby, took the first elevator and exited onto Adams Street. The sidewalks on this sunny, warm day were crowded with men in shirtsleeves, women without jackets and college kids in shorts going to the downtown campuses of DePaul and Roosevelt Universities.

Scott crossed Dearborn heading west, leaving the two agents behind. He looked over his shoulder and saw them standing on the corner of Dearborn and Adams. He kept walking, crossed Clark, and turned north on LaSalle, where he noticed a man in a trench coat. The man had freshly cut dark hair parted on the side, wore black horn-rim glasses and was talking into his wrist. Scott turned into the revolving door of a bank and stood behind the wall next to it.

Ten seconds later the man in the trench coat rushed through the spinning door. Scott grabbed his lapels and turned him so they faced each other. "Tell Richmond and O'Malley they should trust me more than this. You know where I'm going. Why don't you stop for a cup of coffee at Starbucks and I'll meet you there when I'm done."

"I can't do that."

"Come on." Scott reached into his pocket, pulled out a five and slapped it in the agent's palm. "I'll buy."

Scott walked out the door and headed north on LaSalle. Within ten minutes he reached Everson's law firm. He stood outside the door and checked his hands again. Still the slight tremor. He entered the lobby and walked up to the receptionist's window. "Hi, Jeanie."

She swiveled around in her chair. Her eyes looked red and glassy. "Mr. Garity," she whispered. "I think I'm in big trouble."

Scott reached back over his shoulder, as if scratching his neck, and tugged on the microphone cord, pulling it out of the Nagra's jack.

"Can I talk to you?" she asked.

"Sure, I'm fifteen minutes early. Should we go somewhere?"

Jeanie picked up the phone. "Laurie, can you sit in for me for ten minutes?" After a moment she nodded and hung up the phone. "There's a vacant office next door.

Scott followed her into the empty office. She locked the door, then covered her face with both hands and sobbed.

Scott grabbed her shoulders. "Jeanie, what's wrong?"

She lowered her hands. "You know about that man who died at that strip club? Vincent Marchese?"

"I know a little about him. Why?"

"I didn't know it, but he was a client of the firm. I never saw him in the office. When he died, the governor had me pull his client file. The only things in it were powers of attorney for Marchese's bank accounts. The governor had me send the powers of attorney to the banks to put the accounts under my name. I didn't think anything of it. I thought it was temporary until Mr. Marchese's estate was probated."

"Is that something you would ordinarily do?" Scott asked.

She nodded. "Sometimes they put things in my name temporarily. But this time the governor had me write checks payable to different people. People I've never heard of. And then he had me take a cab to a currency exchange on Western Avenue, cash the checks and give the cash to him."

"How much were the checks for?"

"Three checks, each for three thousand dollars." She paused and sniffled. "It's not right. It's not my money, and why did I have to go to a currency exchange on Western Avenue? That's twenty blocks out of the Loop. There are plenty of currency exchanges down here."

"I have an idea why."

"What if he asks me to do it again? I have the check registers. There's over a hundred thousand in the accounts. If I don't do it, I think he'll fire me. I'm a single mother. I can't afford to go a week without a paycheck."

"Give me time. I'll think of something. I can't believe he'd fire you."

"You don't know him like I do." She looked at the floor. "Scott, I...I was having an affair with him. This last month, though, he's been getting more distant. Then Marchese died and he tried to get close again, but it hasn't been the same. I think he realized he needed someone to do whatever it was that Marchese was doing for him. So he came back to me. I figured out he was using me, that there was nothing between us."

Scott frowned. "The last time I talked to him, he said something about having plans for me. Maybe he's thinking I can take Marchese's place and then you'll be off the hook."

She gave him a teary-eyed look. "Please help me, Scott."

"I'm supposed to meet him in a few minutes. Let's see what goes on and I'll let you know." Scott pulled a business card and a pen out of his shirt pocket. "Write your cell phone number on here and I'll get back to you."

She wrote the information on the card and handed it back to Scott.

He tucked it into his pocket. "Wait here for a few minutes so we don't show up at your desk at the same time. Don't worry, everything's going to be all right."

Chapter 29

Everson's Law Office

Scott walked up to Laurie at the receptionist's window and gave her his name. "Can you let the Governor know I'm here to see him?"

"Let that man in." Scott looked up. Everson stood in the doorway that separated the lobby from his firm's inner sanctum. He walked over, grinning broadly, and put his arm around Scott's shoulders. "Laurie, let me introduce you to the Governor's man. I have a feeling you're going to be seeing a lot of him around here." Everson eyed Scott. "I bet you've got good news for me, don't you? Let's go to my office and you can tell me all about it."

They walked down the hallway into Everson's office, where he closed the door behind them. "Sit down and tell me what your snitch had to say." He walked around his massive desk and plopped into the oversized black leather chair.

"I met with my informant and his friend about eleven last night," Scott said. "These guys are night creatures. My CI's friend is a drug user. That's why he was in the drug house and saw Marti."

The ex-governor edged forward in his chair and braced his elbows on his desk. "What'd he say?"

"Late last Tuesday night or early Wednesday morning, he was in the building at 206 N. Kildare getting high. Users go there to buy and shoot up. He bought a couple of dime bags of heroin and did his thing. While he's there, this white girl comes in. He said she was good-looking but strung out, needed a hit bad."

"Did he identify the picture I gave you?"

"He did better than that. I brought several photos from lineups I've used in the past and he picked your girl out right away. Not a moment's hesitation."

"So that proves she was there. Anything else?"

Scott smiled. "Yeah. Apparently, somewhere along the line she picked up a roll of cash."

Everson smacked his hands together. "I knew it. What did he say?"

"You've got to picture this place. There's junkies laid out all over, floating through their Never-Never Land. Our guy is a regular at this place. He says he's never seen this girl there before, so he's watching her, thinking they could get high together and do the dirty deed. She buys a handful of dime bags. More than she'd need for the night. Then she pulls a wad of cash out of her pocket, about an inch thick. He starts thinking of rolling her for the money, but the smack kicks in and he's out of it."

Everson clenched his hands together. "You've got to find her, Scott. You've got to get my money."

"Your money?"

He looked flustered, then recovered. "It's money the Russian was going to use for legal fees he owes me."

"He was going to pay your legal fee in cash?"

"You learn when you're in practice to take a fee any way a client wants to pay it."

"Since it never got to you, isn't it his responsibility to get you the money?"

Everson gave Scott a look like he was asking too many questions. "Your junkie guy say anything else?"

"He said when he came to it was light outside and he saw the girl leaving. He got up because he thought he could follow her and she'd be an easy hit for the cash."

"Where'd she go?"

Scott held Everson's gaze. "That information cost me a thousand bucks."

Everson leaned back in his chair. "Don't play games with me. I told you I'd give you cash." He fished his wallet out of his rear pants pocket, pulled out ten one-hundred dollar bills and tossed them on his desk.

Scott picked them up, folded the bills in half and tucked them away.

"Well?" Everson said.

"She hopped in a car with a West Side pimp."

"He know the pimp's name?"

"Yes."

Everson scowled. "Why do I feel like I'm pulling teeth?"

"Don't worry, I'm tracking this guy down." Scott gave him the name Smithfield had told him. "DeMarcus DeWayne, that's the guy. It should be a matter of a day or two, and then I'll have him and then the girl. What should I do with them?"

"I don't care. Just get my money. Let me check with the Russian and see what he'll pay to get this girl back in his fold."

Scott thought, *you're a classy guy, Governor. I'll play your game.* "By the way, I've used up the retainer you gave me."

Everson unlocked his right-hand desk drawer, lifted out a roll of hundreds and tossed three thousand onto the desk.

Chapter 30

Scott walked out of Everson's law firm onto LaSalle Street. He saw Agent Trench coat leaning against a lamppost under the shadows of the tall buildings, sipping from a Starbucks coffee cup. Scott turned south and the man followed him around the corner, catching up to him on Madison.

"Richmond and O'Malley are waiting for you," Trench coat said.

"You look like a caramel macchiato man. I like mine black. Coulda got one for me."

"I would have, but it would've gotten cold by now."

"You're my escort, I assume?"

"Just keeping you safe and sound."

"How comforting. I didn't catch your name."

"Fred Baxter."

"You must be the new kid on the block. You shave yet?"

They returned to the FBI office on the ninth floor of the Dirksen Federal building, where Baxter badged them past the receptionist and they joined Richmond and O'Malley in the same ten-by-ten interview room. Scott removed his jacket and shirt, and O'Malley stepped behind him to get the Nagra tape recorder.

"What the fuck. The microphone is out of the jack," O'Malley said.

Scott shrugged. "You didn't leave enough loose wire on the cord when you taped it to my shirt. I leaned forward and it must have popped out."

O'Malley's face turned redder that his hair. "Bullshit, you yanked it out."

Scott shook his head. "Yeah, that would make a lot of sense. Play the tape and see what's on it, and I'll fill you in on the rest."

O'Malley pushed the play button and they listened to ten minutes of Scott walking to Everson's office, the wind blowing through the microphone and the swirl of the revolving doors. Then two voices, Scott's and Baxter's:

Tell Richmond and O'Malley they should trust me more than this. You know where I'm going. Why don't you stop for a cup of coffee at Starbucks and I'll meet you there when I'm done.

I can't do that.

Come on, I'll buy.

O'Malley shut off the tape player. "You're a real fucking comedian, Garity. You better watch it. You're walking on thin ice." He turned it back on. They heard the swirl of the revolving door and the wind blowing into the microphone again, then the ping of an elevator when the door opened and once again when it opened on the floor of Everson's law firm. A few seconds later came Scott's voice and then, briefly, Jeanie's:

Hi, Jeanie.

Mr. Garity, I think I'm in big trouble.

The tape went silent.

"That's it. That's all that's on the fucking tape. It's worthless." Eyes narrowed, O'Malley glared at Scott. "What the fuck is she talking about?"

He'd used the few minutes of listening to decide on his story. "That's kind of embarrassing. She said she was in trouble because she had the hots for me."

O'Malley looked furious. "I want you on the phone right now. You call Everson and we'll tape it now."

"I don't think that's a good idea. It'll blow any chance of making a case," Scott said.

"I don't give a damn what you think." O'Malley stabbed a finger at him. "I want you to do exactly what I tell you to do—"

Richmond grabbed O'Malley's hand. "He's right, Red. He calls Everson now and rehashes their conversation, it'll be obvious the whole thing's a set-up. Let Scott tell us what the governor said in response to the scenario we gave him."

"I told him the story exactly the way we discussed," Scott said.

"And?" Richmond asked.

Scott cleared his throat, sat down and folded his hands in front of him. He had to find out if Haller could get an address on the pimp, DeWayne. If Everson gave the pimp's name to the Russian, or Scott gave it to the FBI, the race to get Marti would be on and she'd end up dead— either when the Russian got her or after the FBI made her a witness and a marked woman.

Richmond and O'Malley stood watching him, arms folded over their chests. Baxter leaned against the wall.

Scott looked at Richmond and then O'Malley, hoping he could keep eye contact while he lied to them. "Everson said he didn't know anything about any money Marti had."

"Shit, I don't believe it." O'Malley slammed his hand on the table. "I don't know if it's Everson or you I don't believe."

Scott shrugged. "If you guys are done with me for the day, I'll let myself out."

"We'll be in touch. Baxter, escort out friend out," Richmond said.

Scott left the FBI offices and drove west on the Eisenhower Expressway. He picked up his cell phone and called Haller. "Joe, it's Scott. Any luck on the address for DeWayne?"

"It's not looking good. The El Dorado Cadillac comes back to a Martha Jordan, age fifty-five, lives on Central Avenue a couple blocks north of Madison. I figure she must be the pimp's mother. There's also a Harley and a '63 Mustang convertible registered to her. Absolutely nothing registered under his name."

"Damn it. He pimps girls for a living and pimps his mother to hide his assets."

"Yeah, he's one of a kind." Haller paused. "I missed you at the AA meeting yesterday. Saved a seat for you, but you were a no show."

"Just after I hung up the phone with you I got a visit from those same two FBI agents. Okay if I drop by in half an hour? I'll tell you the rest when I get there."

"See you then."

Chapter 31

Everson left his office and took the elevator down to the first floor. To the right of the elevators were four phone booths. He stepped into the first one, closed the door and emptied the change from his pocket onto a shelf below the telephone. He picked up the receiver, dropped a quarter into the coin slot and dialed the number.

"Yeah."

"This is the King. I need to meet with you tonight. I think that man I told you about might find your girl soon. I'll tell you more at eight tonight. The same parking lot as last time. I'll be in that Chevy again." He hung up and took the elevator back to his office.

Everson entered the lobby, walked up to the receptionist's window and leaned on the frame. Jeanie turned from her typewriter and looked at him. He felt her eyes burning into his, but didn't care. He winked at her. "Could you come to my office for a minute?"

She paused. "I'm really busy. I have to finish this motion for Jack for his trial."

Everson stepped aside and opened the door to the law offices, then returned to her desk and whispered. "This won't take long. I miss you. We haven't had time alone together for a while. Come on." He stepped toward his office. She rose from her chair and followed.

The door to his office was open. He stepped inside and held the door until she entered, then closed it. "You look really nice today."

She gave him a cool look. "What is it you want, James?"

He stepped closer and put his hands on her hips.

Jeanie took a step back.

That was a surprise. He thought fast. "I'm sorry, Jeanie. You probably feel like I've been ignoring you. Things at home have been pretty bad lately." He glanced down. "In fact, Katherine is moving out this weekend." His hands fell to his sides. "I've been so occupied with this situation, I know I haven't given you the attention you deserve. Will you go out to dinner with me tonight?"

Jeanie grabbed his right hand in both of hers. "She's moving out? Are you getting a divorce?"

"She already has an attorney."

She moved one hand to his shoulder and gazed into his eyes. "I'm sorry, James. I should have known something was bothering you. What time?"

"How about if we meet at Edward's? That restaurant on Mannheim Road, say about six-thirty at the private booth in the back."

"Do you think one of these days you'll be able to pick me up at my house?"

He smiled. "I look forward to when we can be seen in public, but I can't do that now. If people saw us and this got to my wife's attorney, it would be brutal."

"I understand." She stood on her toes and kissed his cheek. "I'll make the reservation." He watched her bustle off to her desk with a smile on her face.

Chapter 32

Scott pulled into Haller's driveway and got out of his car. He went to the rear door and saw Haller through the window, washing dishes at the sink. Scott rapped on the window.

Haller came to the door and opened it. "The fibbies can't leave you alone."

"That's just the tip of the iceberg." They sat at the kitchen table and Scott told him the entire story. The monitored telephone call to Everson to set up the meeting for today and then the reason he'd pulled the plug on the tape recorder. "The last thing I wanted to do was get Jeanie in trouble. Everson must have been laundering money through some accounts Marchese set up. After Marchese died, the Gov had Jeanie transfer the accounts into her name, cash checks drawn on the accounts at some currency exchange on the West Side, and give the cash to him. He's fucking her over, literally and figuratively."

"You mean…"

"Yeah, she told me."

"What an asshole." Haller shook his head.

"There's more. The agents told me Marti had twenty grand on her when she ran away from the strip joint."

"So what did the Gov say about the money?"

"He claimed it was for legal fees the Russian owed him. But I fucked up. I told him the pimp's name. Going cold turkey is messing with my head. If they find him, they'll find her."

"And then she's dead," Haller said. "So we don't know where he lives. We can't just sit up on the West Side and hope we see him."

"I've got an idea. It's a long shot, but she came through for me before. I had this informant that was a madam. I haven't talked to her in about two years."

Haller's forehead furrowed. "She on the West Side?"

"No, she's white, was raised in Lake Forest or Kenilworth, something like that. Went through boarding school, white glove cotillions, and some private East Coast college until she dropped out halfway through. She was bored with it. Didn't want to become her mother. She loved the fast life, Rush Street and cocaine cowboys, and made a living with the only skills she learned. Started as an independent call girl, had a lot of contacts on the street and grew her business into an escort service."

"How'd you hook up with her?"

Scott laughed. "Hookup isn't the right word. Had a buddy that worked Vice at the CPD. He introduced me to her, and there was some chemistry there."

"You do the dirty deed with her?"

"I'm sure I could have. Not bragging, but when we were in touch I was married. Kept telling her that, and that it would be unprofessional even if I wasn't. Probably would have got my ass fired."

"Mister Goody Two-shoes. She do you any good?"

"Yeah, she had the kind of clientele we're always interested in—dope dealers, politicians, judges, mob guys, executives, you name it. One time she told me about a loan shark that was trying to duck a grand jury subpoena. He was living at his sister's house. I gave the information to the agents working that case and they laid the paper on him. Another time, a guy on the Board of Education was getting kickbacks from a computer company selling computers to the board that were never graced by a student's fingers. And there was plenty more like that."

"What was in it for her?"

"At first I think she figured there was some insurance being a snitch for a fed. But after a while she wanted more. Then my thing happened in South Hampton and you know the rest of the story."

"So let me figure this out. You're not married anymore and you're not a fed, and as far as I know you haven't had any for a while. So…" Haller raised both hands, palms up.

"Don't jump to conclusions."

"Oh, excuse me. Strictly business. I get it. So how do we get in touch with her?"

"I've got her personal cell number, assuming she hasn't changed it. It's not the one the johns call."

Haller nodded. "Let's do it."

Scott flipped open his cell phone, found the address-book entry for Ashley Fontana and hit the button.

When she answered, her voice was as deep and throaty as he remembered. "Hello."

"Hi, guess who this is?"

"I don't play games. Tell me who you are and who gave you this number, or I'll hang up in three seconds."

"You always were direct. It's Scott."

"Scott…Scotty G.?"

"The one and only."

"I must have called you at least once a month for over a year. All they ever told me was bullshit. He's out of town. He can't be reached right now. We'll leave a message for him. Were you on some top-secret assignment? Oh, never mind. I know you can't tell me."

"If you have some free time, I'd like to see you."

"That can be arranged. There's a Starbucks on Division. It's just two blocks from my house. Say eight?"

"See you there." Scott flipped his phone closed.

Haller smiled. "I think you're in for one hell of a night."

Chapter 33

Edward's Restaurant
Monday, 6:30 PM

EVERSON STEPPED THROUGH THE FRONT door of the restaurant. He wore a wide-brim fedora pulled low over his face and a black leather jacket with the collar turned up. He approached the maître'd. "Is she here, Eddie?"

"Yes, sir, at your favorite booth. Shall I take you there?"

"No, that's fine." Everson palmed him a fifty and walked toward the back of the restaurant to a booth with floor-to-ceiling curtains that shielded the customers from anyone's view. At the moment, the curtains were partway open. The booth was upholstered in red leather, the table dark wood. A dimly lit wall sconce and a candle in a glass holder on the table created a soft light.

Everson slid into the booth. He removed his jacket, folded it, laid it on the seat next to him and put his fedora on top of it. Jeanie was already there, seated across from him. Her face glowed in the flickering light, the curve of her breast visible in her low-cut black silk blouse. A gold chain hung around her neck. It held a heart-shaped medallion with a diamond in the center.

"Hi, sweetie. I'm so glad you agreed to have dinner with me tonight," Everson said.

"I'm so glad you asked me." She smiled and caressed the medallion. "I'm wearing the birthday present you gave me."

"It looks beautiful on you."

Their waiter appeared at the curtain gap. "Good evening, sir," he said, laying menus and a wine list on the table. "Would you like a drink before dinner?"

"No, thank you. We'll have the chateaubriand, medium, with the 1993 cabernet sauvignon."

"Two excellent choices, if I may say so." He backed away from the table and left them alone.

Everson drew the curtains shut. "So tell me, how's everything going with you?" he asked.

"Sometimes the girls can be a challenge. They're already thinking about boys. I can't imagine what it will be like when they start to date." She reached out across the table, one hand toward him.

Everson took it. "Your skin is so soft."

She looked down at their intertwined hands. "Thank you."

The waiter came with the wine and separated the curtain. He set two glasses down on the table, uncorked the bottle and poured an ounce into Everson's glass.

Everson let go of Jeanie's hand, picked up the glass and swirled the wine around in it, admiring its color and texture. Then he took a sip, swished the wine in his mouth and swallowed. "Excellent." He put the glass down. The waiter filled both glasses and rested the bottle on the table, then gracefully withdrew.

"I hope things haven't been too stressful at work?" Everson said.

"No, not bad. I was more worried about us."

"I'm sorry. I hope you understand what's been going on. I prefer not to discuss it tonight." Everson smiled. "I just want to have a wonderful time, like we usually do."

Jeanie smiled back. "Me, too."

They chatted for the next fifteen minutes and then the steaks were served. By the time they finished the main course, it was seven forty-five.

"Honey, do you mind if I borrow your car for a little while? You can have your crème bruleé, and I should be back by eight-fifteen at the latest. Then we can have a nightcap at our favorite little hideaway."

"Where're you going?"

"It's just business. You know I can never stop working."

She gave a puzzled frown. "Are you going to meet Mr. Garity?"

He laughed. "No. Why do you ask?"

"He seems like a really nice guy. Are you going to be employing him regularly?"

"Could be. I like him, too. I call him my man. I guess I'll be using him on anything special that comes up. I feel I can trust him."

"That's good. I trust him, too," Jeanie said, wiping her lips with her napkin. "I told him about the checks I cashed for you at the currency exchange."

"You…" he paused as he tried to cover his shock. He couldn't afford to let her see it right now. "We have to protect the privacy of our clients. In the future, you shouldn't tell him things like that." He glanced down at his wine glass. *Son of a bitch, what do I do with him now?*

Chapter 34

Starbucks, Division and Dearborn
Tuesday, 8:00 PM

SCOTT STEPPED INTO THE COFFEE shop wearing a beige turtleneck sweater over jeans and brown loafers. The aroma of Ethiopian Sidamo hung in the air and the chatter of twenty conversations backed by the soft sounds of Joni Mitchell's *Chelsea Morning* filled the room. The line of customers was eight deep. Every table was taken, people reading books and magazines, tapping their laptop keyboards, planning their weekend agendas and getting a load of caffeine before hitting the bars for a long night. But there was no sign of Ashley.

He joined the line and listened to the orders, ranging from venti half-caf frappuccinos to grande cinnamon lattes, and pondered if ordering a plain black coffee would cause a halt to the whole process. In five minutes he was up to third in line when he felt an elbow in his back as someone brushed against him.

He jerked his head around and saw her. Shoulder-length blonde hair, parted in the center, shaded over the right side of her face. The soft lights made her blue eyes sparkle. She had high cheek bones, a little nose, gleaming white teeth surrounded by red lips. She was approaching forty but it was obvious from her tight-fitting black leather pants that she still exercised five days a week. She wore a black leather waist-length jacket, unbuttoned, revealing a silver sequined sweater with a deep V-neck.

"Excuse me, sir," she said, as if she didn't know him.

Scott realized she was in one of her game-playing moods and went with it. "I'm sorry, did I take your place in line?"

"Why yes, you did." She placed a hand on his shoulder. "But you can make it up to me and buy me a vanilla latte. Oh, look, that couple over there is leaving. Just bring it to me at the table." She turned and walked away, most of the men eyeing the saunter of her stride until she sat down.

A few minutes later, Scott joined her, put down her drink and sat. "You should've been an actress."

"I always have been, just for private audiences. Thanks. " She picked up the cup, took a sip and put it down. "You still married?"

"Why do you want to know?"

"Just catching up, it's been such a long time." She crossed her legs.

He brought his cup to his lips and sipped coffee.

"Well, are you or aren't you?"

"No, I'm not. But you can't blame her. Can you imagine what it must've been like being married to me? All those crazy hours."

"I can't imagine what it would be like being married to anyone. Do you still see your ex?"

"No, she moved up to Michigan. That's where she was from. But I've got our son."

"He must be a teenager by now."

"Almost. He's with our family priest. Comes over to the house and watches videos with Billy."

"So you're free for the night." It was more statement than question.

"Business has been good. Last month I bought a three-flat in Bucktown."

"Business must be booming."

"You not working for the IRS now, are you?"

He laughed. "No."

"Even if you were, I'm not worried. My accountant and lawyer have my escort service set up as Ashley's Private Collection, a subchapter S corporation. I save some tax dollars that way and report enough income to cover my living expenses. So even if you were IRS, I wouldn't have to worry about it." She folded her arms across her chest, turned her head, looked out the window and then back at Scott, straight into his eyes. "You're not telling me much. I assume you're still with the government and I'm still just your snitch."

"I'm sorry, I didn't call you to upset you."

"Why did you call?"

"I'm not with the feds anymore."

"You quit? I thought you were God's gift to the government."

"No, I didn't quit. I was shot last January. I've been off duty since then. I still have a bullet in my spine. They put me on disability because they think I'm too much of a liability risk."

She uncrossed her legs, reached across the table and covered Scott's hand. "Scott, I'm so sorry. I didn't know. I called your office and your cell phone almost every month and they never told me anything."

He saw the diamond-encrusted bezel of her Rolex peeking out from her jacket sleeve. "They said what they were supposed to."

"So, are you all right?"

"I'm as good as I'm going to be. Sometimes my back hurts a little. I pop a pill and keep on moving." He glanced out the window. *Not going to tell you I'm in N.A.*

"So why did you call?"

"There's a young girl in trouble. I know you have a lot of contacts and I was hoping you might be willing to help her."

Ashley cocked her head. "What's this girl to you?"

"I'm a private investigator now. My client hired me to find her."

"I don't understand. How could I help you?"

"You could help me and possibly help yourself."

"How's that?"

"My client is former governor Everson. You'd be doing him a big favor if you help me find her and I'm sure the Governor would be very thankful. If you should ever need a favor…you know how things work in this state."

She sighed. "So how can I help?"

"This girl, her name is Martina Zicek, she goes by the name Marti. She's from Europe. Her parents sent her here to get an education. She got involved with the wrong people and the last we know of her, she became an exotic dancer at a place known as the Pole Club out on Mannheim Road. Last Tuesday night she ran away from the club with twenty grand in cash. She has a tattoo of a dragon on her back. She was last seen on the West Side last Wednesday morning when she left with a pimp named DeMarcus Dewayne. Ever hear of him?"

He looked into her eyes and saw she was weighing the pros and cons of helping him.

"I don't know many black pimps." She swallowed. "I don't know this guy DeMarcus and I don't deal with streetwalkers."

Scott pulled the photo of Marti out of his back pocket and slid it across the table. "She's only eighteen. As you can see from her photo, she's very pretty. I don't think a guy like DeWayne would put her on the street when she could make a lot more money with higher-class johns. Could you check around? See if you can find out where I can find him…or her."

"I could do that, but I can't guarantee anything."

Scott could see the disappointment in her eyes. He reached out and took her hand.

"Is that all you want?" she asked.

"The strip joint belongs to Drazen Ivanov, a Russian mobster. He's looking for her too, and if he finds her first I'm afraid he'll kill her."

"I told you I don't know the pimp. So don't get your hopes up." She grabbed the photo, looked at it and stood up. "She's not that pretty. I don't know if I'd use her. I'll call you." She turned and left the coffee shop.

Chapter 35

Tuesday, 8:00 PM

Everson pulled up next to Drazen's Lexus in the grocery store parking lot and rolled down the window. "Hop in, we'll go for a ride."

The Russian got out of his car and entered the passenger side of the Chevy Malibu. Everson pulled away from the Lexus and parked on the far side of the lot.

"Not a very long ride." Drazen lifted a Macanudo out of his shirt pocket and stuck it in his mouth.

"That shiny car of yours might attract attention. That's why I borrow this shit bucket. No one will notice it." Everson pulled his fedora lower over his face.

Drazen pushed the button on his Calibri torch lighter. The flame jetted up and he held it under the tip of the cigar. "So your man has a lead on my Marti?" As he inhaled, the tip of the cigar glowed red and a cloud of smoke drifted up.

"One of his informant's friends saw the girl leaving a drug house on the West Side—"

Drazen whipped the cigar out of his mouth. "What the fuck. I know all about that. That's where I sent my son to his death chasing that whore and your dirty money."

Everson raised his hands, palms down. *Need to placate this son of a bitch.* "Drazen, I know and I'm sorry you lost your son. I can't imagine how terrible that must have been for you."

Drazen put the cigar back between his lips and whispered. "And my brother, all on the same fuckin' night."

"This is your chance to get revenge against the bitch that caused your son's death." He handed the Russian a copy of Scott's identification photo with his address written on the back.

"What's this for?"

"That's my man, Scott Garity, and his address. His informant's friend gave him the lead. He said he should be able to find the girl in a day or two. If you have some good men that could follow him, he'll lead you to the girl and you can do with her as you please."

"And what about the twenty thousand?"

"Unfortunately, my man Garity has learned too much. If you take care of him when you get the girl, I'll consider that your fee and we'll be even."

The Russian smirked, drew the cigar from his mouth, and pointed it at the governor as if saluting as he left the car. "*Na zdorovie.*" Cheers.

Chapter 36

Tuesday, 8:15 PM

ASHLEY WALKED TWO BLOCKS NORTH on the east side of Dearborn Parkway. She was torn between her anger for feeling Scott was using her again, just like when he was an agent, and the thought in the back of her mind that getting Marti for him could bring Scott to her. She walked up the stairs of her two-story greystone, took the key out of her jacket pocket and unlocked the front door.

She stepped into the foyer, flicked on the light switch for the chandelier, and threw her jacket onto a small telephone table against the wall. It slid off. She kicked it across the hardwood floor and picked up the telephone receiver. "Son of bitch, I don't believe it." She punched in a number and put the receiver to her ear.

"Yeah," a man's voice answered.

"DeMarcus, what time is the first date tonight?"

"Ten."

"Who're you taking?"

"Mercedes."

"The girl with the tattoo?"

"Yeah."

"How long before you can meet me at North Avenue and Dearborn?"

"I'm not far away, can be there in fifteen minutes."

"See you there." Ashley hung up. She picked up her jacket and walked into her living room, turning on a lamp as she headed toward the bar. She grabbed a glass, reached into an ice bucket and snagged a handful of ice cubes, dropped them into her glass and filled it with Amaretto. She tossed her jacket across the white leather couch and looked at her reflection in the mirror hanging over the fireplace. "This is not going to turn out well, stuck between the ex-governor, a Russian mobster, twenty grand, that little whore, and Scott. What does she mean to him anyway?"

She pushed her hair off her face and paced in front of the mirror, draining her drink and chewing the ice. *If I help Scott, will that really help me? If the Russian finds her, DeMarcus will probably be there too. They'll kill him. Then I'll have to find a new delivery boy.* She filled her glass again and collapsed on the couch.

Scott stood in the darkness of the stairwell to the garden apartment opposite Ashley's greystone. A light in the living room went on and he could see her silhouette behind the curtains, walking back and forth. Five minutes later the light went off. The front door opened. Scott moved further back in the stairwell. He saw Ashley come down the stairs and walk north.

He waited ten seconds, then jogged up to the sidewalk and stayed on the west side of the street, fifty feet behind her. He felt undetected, shielded behind the bumper-to-bumper parked cars and the trees on the parkway. She walked at a brisk pace with a definite purpose. He knew it wasn't a casual evening stroll.

She stopped at the end of the first corner, Burton Place, and looked behind her.

Scott bent down, pretending to tie his shoes even though he was wearing loafers. When he stood up, she was still on the corner. He stepped onto the parkway and leaned against a tree. Couples strolled past him heading south to the bars and restaurants in the area of Division and Rush. He glanced around the tree. She was still standing there, hands on hips, apparently staring in his direction. He half-expected her to come running across the street to give him a tongue-lashing. He took a deep breath and glanced around the tree again. She was off the corner.

Scott looked south to see if she was heading back home. Nothing. That left north, east or west. He quickened his pace to the corner and looked east and west. No sign of her. *Must be going north, or she ducked into a building on Burton Place.*

He headed north up Dearborn Parkway, still on the west side of the street. Halfway up the block was group of people getting out of two double-parked cars, a stretch limousine and a Mercedes 600 convertible. The crowd blocked his view of the sidewalk. He picked up his pace. *Damn it, I lost her.*

He broke into a slow jog. Three buildings south of North Avenue, he spotted her and stopped. She was standing in the glass-enclosed lobby of the high rise on the southeast corner of North Avenue and Dearborn Parkway. She glanced at her watch. *She must be waiting for someone.*

Scott looked at his Casio. *Eight thirty-eight.*

He hid behind a lamp post and tried to look inconspicuous to the people coming in and out of the buildings and heading down the sidewalk. *I bet I've got no more than ten minutes before a squad pulls over because someone thinks I'm casing a joint.*

He glanced at his watch again. *Eight forty-three.*

He looked around the lamppost and saw an older black El Dorado convertible in mint condition pull into the circular drive in front of the high rise. Ashley pushed through the revolving doors of the condo building and hopped into the El Dorado's passenger seat. The pimp, he guessed. He could just see Ashley through the rear window as the car idled in the driveway. *The way she's waving her arms she not happy with you, DeMarcus.*

Chapter 37

"You said you'd be here by eight-thirty. You think I've nothing better to do than wait around for you?" Ashley pulled the photo of Marti out of her jacket pocket and tossed it at him. "Is this her?"

DeMarcus lifted the photo from his lap. "That's Marti. She doing good." His brow wrinkled. "What's wrong?"

"Everybody wants her ass. That's what's wrong. Apparently she was good little girl that went wild. Her parents sent her here from Europe to get an education. She got an education, all right, working at strip joint on Mannheim Road. She stole twenty G's from the club and now she's working for us. The problem is, the owner of the strip joint wants his money back. He's a Russian mobster and her parents are represented by James Everson. In case you're not up on politics, he's the former governor of Illinois. And I just met with the guy he hired to find Marti. He's a former federal agent. Otherwise, everything is fucking fine."

DeMarcus leaned against his door. "Oh shit. What do we do?"

"We? You're the one that brought her in."

"Maybe you can give me that fed's number. I can call him and play dumb. He mentions your name, I don't know you." He shook his head. "Tell him I heard on the West Side that he's been lookin' for her and I can bring her in, or tell him where she be."

"Hm, that's not too bad." She raised her eyebrows.

He shrugged. "This girl don't know your name. Keeps you out of it all the way."

Ashley rubbed her forefinger over her chin. *Do I want to be out of it all the way? I could tell Scott I put the word out and he should be getting a call.* "Let me think about it and I'll get back to you tomorrow. When will you be seeing her next?"

"Tonight. She's got a date."

"Be careful. Who knows what these Russians might do."

He frowned. "One thing I don't get. You said she stole twenty grand from the Russian. I picked her up last Wednesday morning in front of a drug house on the West Side. Everything she had, she carried wrapped up in her arms. We been spending time together since. You know what I mean. If she had that kind of cash, I would've seen it."

"I'm just telling you what I've been told. Don't tell her anything. I'll think things over tonight and call you in the morning. And one more thing." She waggled her finger in his face. "Don't ever be fucking late for a meeting with me again."

"Yes, ma'am."

"Drive me home."

Chapter 38

Scott watched the El Dorado pull out of the circular drive and head east on North Avenue. He ran to the corner and saw the Cadillac turn south on the next street, North State Parkway. His car was parked five blocks away. *Damn it. No way I can get there in time to follow them.*

He turned around and walked south on Dearborn Parkway. *Do I go back to the brownstone across from Ashley's and wait?*

As the night grew later, more of the beautiful people thronged the sidewalks. He wove between couples leaving their high-rise condos and crossing his path as they stepped into cabs, limos, Beamers and Benzes. Others entered the high rises and greystones heading to parties and dinners where you had to know someone to get an invitation. He crossed Burton Place and saw a car slowing a half-block down. Its red brake lights flooded the street behind it, and a moment later the passenger door opened.

Ashley. Scott rushed down the sidewalk and bumped into a couple in their priciest designer garb. "Hey, you son of a bitch," the man shouted after him. Scott ignored him and kept going. He saw Ashley climb the stairs to her greystone, unlock the door and go inside.

The El Dorado headed north.

Scott was three car lengths ahead of it on the sidewalk. He lunged between a parked Porsche 911 and an Audi.

The El Dorado was a car away. The Porsche pulled away from the curb and the Cadillac screeched to a stop.

Scott ran up and smacked the hood of the Caddy with the flat of his hand. "Get out of the car."

The black man driving it lunged back in his seat, as if he'd heard a gunshot. He stared at the Porsche in front of him. The sports car's engine sputtered and died.

Scott stepped to the driver's-side window of the El Dorado and kicked it with the heel of his shoe. The window glass broke in a spiderweb pattern. "Get outta the fuckin' car."

The Porsche's engine screamed as its tires ripped into the pavement and the car fishtailed up the street.

The black man punched the accelerator and the Caddy followed the Porsche.

The sudden move spun Scott against the side of the car and threw him to the pavement. His jeans ripped at the knee and his right palm scraped against the asphalt. He picked himself up off the street and glared at the shrinking taillights of the El Dorado as it sped further north. "Fucking son of a bitch." He brushed dirt and bits of gravel off his hands, then turned and faced the greystone.

A light flashed on in the living room. Scott ran across the street, up the stairs and banged on the door. "Open the damn door, Ashley."

The door opened a crack. Scott jabbed it, forcing it wide. The force threw Ashley backward a few steps. She stood there in a white terry-cloth robe. "You're bleeding. What happened to you?"

Scott's nostrils flared, his chest rising and falling with anger and adrenaline rush. "Why'd you lie to me?"

"Come to the bathroom. You need your hand and knee cleaned and bandaged." She turned to go upstairs.

Scott grabbed the back of her robe collar. "Damn it, why'd you lie?"

She spun around, and the robe slipped off.

Scott held it and looked at her. She wore a black lace bra and matching panties. His animal instincts roiled in his mind. Heat rushed through his chest to his loins.

She stepped toward him, hesitating as if she feared rejection.

He kissed her, felt the heat rise within him and sweat breaking down his back and chest. DeMarcus and Marti became distant thoughts.

Ashley pulled his turtle neck off and laid her palms flat on his naked chest.

Scott felt his heart pounding against her hands. He felt her tongue exploring his.

She grabbed his hand and led him to the white leather sofa in the living room. She dropped her bra and panties to the floor.

He kicked off his shoes and she pulled down his jeans and boxers.

He leaned into her and they lay back on the couch. Her hands caressed the muscles in his arms and slid down over his buttocks. He entered her and she arched her back. Her fingernails raked his torso. He thrust again and again and she bit down on the skin of his shoulder until they lay there drenched in sweat and exhaustion.

Scott sat up and reached for his boxers.

Ashley stood, picked up her underwear and walked to the foyer for her robe. "I'll get us drinks. What would you like?"

He slipped on his jeans. "Coke or ginger ale would be fine." He finished dressing, while Ashley slipped on her robe and went to the bar.

She placed a can of Coke on it, then filled a glass with ice and poured herself some amaretto. "Like I asked you before you got carried away, what happened? How'd you get scraped up?"

Scott walked up to the bar and popped open the Coke. "Why'd you lie to me about DeMarcus?"

"What do you mean?"

He took a sip from the can. "I saw you meet him at the high rise on the corner."

She narrowed her eyes. "Are you fucking spying on me?"

"Don't give me that shit. I'm trying to save a girl's life and you know the goddamn pimp that has her, and you lie to me."

Ashley brought her glass to her lips, downed the liquor and crunched on the ice. "I wasn't sure you were talking about the same girl. I had to check it out. Showed him the picture you gave me. It's her."

"Look, I don't want to listen to your bullshit. I just want the girl before the Russian finds her."

"Aren't you the romantic type, fuck me and then tell me I'm a bullshitter. You really know how to get to a girl's heart."

"I'm sorry. The longer it takes me to find her, the greater the chance Drazen Ivanov will and they'll kill her just to make an example of her to the other girls he's got working for him." He told her about following the van from the Pole Club to the apartment that was like a prison, and then the black Mercedes to the Russian's lakefront mansion.

"Okay, I'll help you. But DeMarcus won't be able to see her until tomorrow. He's got things to do tonight."

"I'll call you tomorrow, first thing." He walked to the foyer, grabbed his turtle neck off the floor and slipped it on.

"Where're you going?"

"I've got to go home."

"I thought you'd spend the night."

"I've got a son to take care of."

She walked up to Scott, slipped a finger in one of his belt loops and tugged it. "I'm sure you can trust that priest to take care of him."

"That's not the point. He's my son and I told him I'd be home in a couple of hours."

She pulled him closer, so they were chest to chest. "Use my phone. Tell him something came up." She laughed.

"I said I'll call you tomorrow."

"You're no fun." She grabbed a pen off the table, wrote her personal land-line number on a business card for Ashley's Private Collection and handed it to him. "Now you've got all my numbers."

Chapter 39

Tuesday, 9:45 PM

DeMarcus gave Marti a sidelong glance as she slipped into the passenger seat of the El Dorado. She wore a red dress that was molded to her body and stopped at mid-thigh, with a matching handbag and red stiletto heels. He drove south on Sheridan Road and then Lake Shore Drive, and exited onto Michigan Avenue.

"You're quiet tonight," she said.

"Sorry, guess I'm not in a good mood. Had an argument with the boss lady."

"What was she upset about?" She crossed her legs. The dress crawled higher on her thigh.

"Ah, she was having trouble with a client or maybe one of the girls and she got pissed at me 'cause I was late meeting her."

"You shouldn't take it personally. Am I ever going to meet her?"

"That wouldn't be smart business. You in demand, and she might try to cut me out."

"I wouldn't let that happen. You saved me, DeMarcus." She slid over to him and draped her arm around his shoulders.

"Baby, you know you're special to me. From that first time I saw you, I knew I had to have you. In this business you have to keep things in a certain order or it just gets…confusing."

"Where're you taking me?"

"We almost there?" He turned east off of Michigan Avenue and went down two blocks. The street was much darker than the Magnificent Mile. He pulled to the curb. "Here, baby, Room 404."

Marti pushed the door open. She put one foot on the curb and looked up at the red neon sign—H *tel Internationale*, with the missing o—and slid back into the seat. "I can't go in there."

"Come on, baby. You got a paying customer waiting on you."

She closed the door. "I can't, DeMarcus."

"Don't be acting up. You get your ass up there. Man's waiting and he's paid up."

"I can't."

He put his hand on the back of her neck. "Look, I already had words with the boss lady tonight. You go up there or I'll have more of her shit to deal with." He tightened his grip.

She jerked her neck free and looked him in the eye. "DeMarcus, when you left me here the other night. It got bad. I hit the guy with a bottle of vodka."

He let out a breath. "Honey, those things are going to happen once in a while. I'm sorry. You should've told me. I would've gone up there and punched the asshole out. Nobody's going to hurt my Marti." He loosened his grip and massaged her neck.

"I can't go in there."

"This a different john. He be sweet as a honey bear."

"That other guy, I think I killed him."

His hand fell away from her. "Fuck, girl, why you first be telling me this now?"

"That Russian I ran away from, it was his brother. I was scared. I didn't know it until he saw my dragon tattoo and he said he saw me at his brother's club. What could I do? He'd tell him, and then Drazen would know how to find me. I took some money the night I left the club. The only reason I took it was because I wanted to get clean. I don't have the money any more. Someone at that drug house stole it from me when I was high. He'll kill me for sure."

DeMarcus leaned against the window. "Motherfucker, Ashley was right."

Chapter 40

Wednesday, 11:00 AM

SCOTT CALLED ASHLEY. "I WANT to make arrangements so I can talk to Marti. You have any suggestions?"

"How nice of you to call me after our romantic interlude last night. Are you going to send me flowers too?"

"Ashley we're getting down to the zero hour. We don't have much time to take care of this situation before it deteriorates into a real mess. We need to put all our attention to getting Marti out of harm's way."

"I don't get it. What's in this for you?"

"I don't like to see people victimized, and even more, I hate the abusers. I'll have a hard time living with myself if she gets hurt because I didn't do what needed to be done."

"Jesus, Scott. Victims, abusers—you sound like you know what you're talking about. You should've been a shrink."

Scott said nothing, just shook his head.

"Are you still there?" she asked.

"I would appreciate if you would work with me on this."

Ashley exhaled. "All right, I'll call DeMarcus and get a feel for, as you call it, 'the situation' and get back to you in an hour. Is that okay, Special Agent Garity? Oh, pardon me, you're only an ordinary citizen now."

"That would be fine, Ashley."

During the next hour Scott received a call from Agent Richmond but let it go to voicemail. "Scott, it's William Richmond, FBI. Please call me as soon as you can."

Shortly afterward, Ashley called. "Do you want the scoop, agent?"

How long will she play this game? "Yeah, give me the scoop."

"Our girl stole the Russian's money because she was going to use it to get clean."

"What'd she do with it?"

"Apparently the Russians kept control of the dancers by shooting them up with heroin every night. As fate would have it, the night she ran away she started going through withdrawal and needed a fix. She hopped in a cab and the driver took her to a drug house on the West Side. She got her fix, but some junkie must have lifted the cash from her while she was in la-la land. At least, that's the story she told DeMarcus. That's where DeMarcus said he picked her up."

"That's interesting. She wanted to get clean so bad, she risks her life." He paused a moment and thought. "We need a place to meet DeMarcus and Marti where she'll be comfortable going. Otherwise she might think we're the Russians coming to get her."

"He said she likes reggae. That's the music she picked to dance to at the strip joint. There's a club on Halsted, a couple of blocks north of Fullerton."

"Tell DeMarcus to have her there tonight at eight." A beep sounded in his ear, indicating an incoming call. He looked at the display. It read *unknown*. Richmond again, Scott figured. *The G's numbers must be encrypted.* He decided to let it go to voicemail again.

"Hello, you still there?" Ashley said.

"Yeah, sorry."

"Scott, maybe you haven't been out much lately. You get there at eight, you might be the only ones there. The band won't start until later."

"All right, a full house might be better. We can hide in the crowd. What time would be good?"

"I'd say not earlier than ten."

"Okay, make it ten. DeMarcus say anything else about Marti?"

"She told him she was kidnapped in Bosnia two years ago, when she was sixteen. Forced into the sex trade, and then the Russian bought her and smuggled her here."

"That's a lot different from the Gov's bullshit story. Her hell started when she was sixteen, unreal." He shook his head. "Make sure she's at the club at ten, call me back to confirm."

"Yes, sir, Mr. Agent."

The line went silent. Scott shut off his phone and walked to the living-room window. A half-block north on the opposite side of the street he saw a white work van parked. *I bet Richmond is sitting in that van steaming mad at me because I'm not answering his calls.*

Drazen Ivanov sat in a chair in the rear of the van, peering through its darkened rear windows at Scott's house. He lifted binoculars to his eyes and saw the man standing in the front window. He glanced down at the photo of Scott the ex-governor had given him. "He's in the house," he said to Luka, who was in the driver's seat. Then he placed a call on his Nextel phone. "Sergei, he's home. We wait for him to move. Are you and Mikhail set?"

"I'm at the south end of the block with a view down the alley so can I see his garage," Sergai said. "Mikhail is at the north end."

Drazen took a moment to picture them. Sergei in the blue Audi, Mikhail in the green Buick Regal. Between them, Scott Garity wouldn't be going anywhere without a tail. "Whoever sees him first let us know so we can follow him to Marti." Drazen said as he adjusted the Makarov PM semi-auto on his hip.

Scott punched a number into his cell phone. Joe Haller answered. "Hello?"

"Joe, it's Scott, I need your help tonight. I think I've got it set up to get Marti. Can you give me a hand?"

"Sure enough. When, where and how?"

"That pimp, DeMarcus DeWayne, is supposed to take her to a reggae club a couple of blocks north of Fullerton on Halsted at ten. Can you meet me there?"

"Sure."

"When you get in the area, call me on my cell. I'll be leaving soon and roaming around the North Side."

"North Side, isn't that where your friend the madam lives?"

"That's where the bar is. Bring your hardware just in case. I'll be up there around nine-thirty."

"See you there."

"One more thing. Richmond from the FBI keeps calling me. Left a voicemail, and I think the FBI might be watching me. There's a van parked down the street. Keep your eyes peeled." He flipped his phone shut.

At five o'clock, Richmond closed his cell phone. He looked at Red O'Malley, who sat in the chair in front of Richmond's desk. "That's the third time I've called Garity since noon. Each time I left a message and he hasn't called me back yet."

"Asshole," O'Malley said.

"He's up to something—like getting Marti now, or if not now, soon."

"Why don't we take a ride to his house? See if he's with us or against us."

"Let's go."

Chapter 41

5:30 PM

SCOTT AND BILLY WALKED OUT the back of the house and into the garage. Scott backed the Olds Cutlass into the alley, got out and closed the garage door, returned to the car and headed south. "I called Father Dugan. He wants to see that movie *Seven Years in Tibet*. How's that sound to you?"

"Sounds boring."

"Brad Pitt is in it. He's pretty good."

"Well, at least Father Dugan likes popcorn. He always gets a large and we get free refills."

"That sounds like fun. I'm probably going to be late tonight, so you can stay at Father Dugan's place. I'll get you in the morning and we'll go out for breakfast." Scott pulled up to the rectory and Billy hopped out of the car. The priest held the front door open and Billy scampered inside. Scott watched him go and then looked for the white van, but it was nowhere to be seen.

At six-fifteen Richmond parked the gray Crown Vic in front of Scott's house. "Let's see if he's trying to avoid us." He knocked on the door while O'Malley went down the gangway to the rear of the house.

Richmond knocked again, harder. There was no response.

O'Malley returned to the front. "Don't waste your energy. His car is gone."

"Son of a bitch. Let's go to Haller's and see if he's there."

Scott fought the bumper-to-bumper rush hour traffic heading east on the Eisenhower Expressway. It was six forty-five by the time he found a spot to park on LaSalle Street two blocks west of Dearborn Parkway. He was walking east on Schiller Street when a white work van passed him. The driver gave him a sidelong glance. *Looks like the van that was by my house. Should have got the license plate,* he thought. He stopped on the corner of Schiller and Dearborn Parkway and waited to see if the van would come around again. After ten minutes of loitering without seeing it, he headed south a block and knocked on the door of Ashley's greystone.

Ashley opened the door. "Nice to see you again," she said and kissed him on the cheek.

He stepped into the foyer and closed the door. "I think the FBI is tailing me."

"You could say 'It's nice to see you too.'"

"One of their agents called me three times today and there was a white work van parked near my house. I just saw one a hell of a lot like it after I parked my car." He went from the foyer to the living room and peeked through the curtains.

She followed him, stopped and put her arm around his shoulders. "You can't put business before pleasure all the time."

"Right now I can."

She dropped her arm and walked to the bar. "What did the agent want?"

"I'm sure he wanted to get together to find out how we could get Marti." He stepped away from the curtain and joined her at the bar.

"You didn't talk to him?" She poured herself an amaretto on the rocks.

"No, he just left messages for me to call him back."

"Why didn't you?"

"Lying to a federal agent is a felony. You're better off saying nothing."

"You want your usual?"

"Coke is good." He left the bar and sat on the sofa.

Ashley filled a tall glass with ice, popped a Coke open, set them down on the coffee table and sat next to Scott. "So what do we do now?"

"Have you heard from DeMarcus?"

"Not yet."

"Call him."

"Don't worry. He does what I tell him to do. I'm his bread and butter."

"Call him."

"He'll be there. Don't' be such a pain."

Richmond drove past Haller's house at six fifty-five.

"There's a Chevy Impala in the driveway," O'Malley said as he lifted the microphone to his mouth and called in the license plate. A minute later the base station called them back with registration on the car.

"That's our man," O'Malley said.

Richmond parked down the block where they had an eyeball on Haller's driveway.

Haller got into his car at seven p.m. and backed out of the driveway, then drove through the winding tree-lined streets of Riverside and headed north on Harlem Avenue toward the Eisenhower Expressway. He glanced in the rearview mirror and saw a gray Crown Vic two cars behind him. He stopped at the red light at Roosevelt Road a couple of blocks south of the expressway. The same car was still behind him. *Shit, better test these guys.*

The light turned green. Haller punched the accelerator, turning east on Roosevelt. A half-block down he saw the Crown Vic in his rearview mirror. *God damn, it's got to be the FBI.*

Four blocks later, he turned south on Oak Park Boulevard and pulled into a parking space in the residential neighborhood lined with brick bungalows and two-flats. He waited, and saw the Crown Vic turn the corner and park behind him.

In his side mirror, Haller saw a black man get out of the Crown Vic and approach. He was wearing a long-sleeved white shirt and blue tie, and a semi-auto on his hip. Haller glanced in the other direction and saw a white man standing next to his passenger door. The man's hand was braced on the butt of a holstered revolver.

Haller rolled down his window. The black man—Richmond, if he recalled right—flashed a badge in his face. "FBI."

"You guys had me worried," Haller said. "I figured someone was tailing me and couldn't figure out why. You never know nowadays, things happen."

Richmond put one hand on the car roof and leaned into the open window. "Come on, Joe. You know why we're here."

"You're the guys that talked to Scott."

"That's right, and we want to talk to him again. But I'm getting the feeling he doesn't want to talk to us."

"What makes you say that?"

"Doesn't matter. Tell me where he is."

Haller pursed his lips. "I tried calling him and he hasn't called me back. He's not feeling well lately. I think he just shut off his cell phone to get some sleep. Look I'm…I'm on my way to an AA meeting. I'm going to be late as it is." He shook his head. "I swear guys, I don't know where he is."

"Joe, I know he talked to you about the Russian and the girl and you did some research for Scott," Richmond said.

The other agent—O'Malley—tapped on the passenger window. Haller pushed the button and it eased down. "Look, Joe, my bet is your buddy is meeting the girl. If he had any smarts, he'd have us along with him. Because the Russians want her bad, and if they find them together it won't be pretty."

Haller pushed his fingers through his hair. "You guys got me worried."

"He told us you're an ex-IRS agent, so you know the ramifications of making a false statement to a fed. You're walking a thin line. I want you to call him," Richmond said.

"Right now? But I'm late for my meeting."

O'Malley opened the passenger door and sat next to Haller. Richmond opened the rear door and slid into the rear seat. "Dial his number and give me the phone," Richmond said.

"Now," O'Malley said.

Haller pulled his cell phone out of his shirt pocket and hit the buttons for Scott's number. O'Malley yanked the phone out of his hand and gave it to Richmond.

Scott's cell trilled. The screen showed Haller's number. "Hi, Joe," Scott said.

"It's Agent Richmond. We're with your buddy."

Scott went tense. "Is there a problem?"

"You tell me. I called you three times, left messages on your voicemail and you never called me back."

"I'm sorry. I've been having trouble with this phone. I took it back to the store and they gave me a new one."

"Scott, don't fuck with us. If you're lying, you know we can prove it."

"I'm sorry. I'm worried about this girl. I've got a lead I'm working on and I promise you if it works out, I'll call you." He hung up.

CHAPTER 12

DeMarcus DeWayne's Apartment
Tuesday, 9:15 PM

SPRAWLED ACROSS THE SILK SHEETS of his king-sized bed, DeMarcus leaned on his palm, and looked at the glow on Marti's face after a passionate lovemaking session. "Hey, baby, I've got a surprise for you. I'm gonna take you to best reggae club in the city tonight. They gonna play all your favorite Bob Marley music." He hopped out of bed and danced toward the bathroom, singing, "'I shot the sheriff, but I did not shoot the deputy.'"

Marti sighed. "You know I worked the last three nights. I think I'd rather stay home and watch a movie."

Oh shit, DeMarcus thought. *I don't get her to the club, Ashley will be bitching forever.* "Come on now, baby. I'll buy you some Cristal and you can get some tasty Jamaican food. You come with me tonight and I promise you I'll take you to Montego Bay when it gets icy fuckin' cold here in January."

She sat up in bed, arched her back and pointed her breasts in his direction. "You should take me anyway. Has anyone ever put more money in your pocket than me?"

"You know I love you and appreciate everything you do for me. This is one more thing I want to do. Take you to this club. You told me reggae was your favorite music to dance to at that club you use to work at."

She scowled. "That's one more reason I don't want to go. I'm not going to do anything that'll remind me of the Russian's club."

I'm in fucking trouble, DeMarcus thought.

"What's so special about going there that I can't top here tonight with you?" She rolled her long legs over the side of the bed and stood there naked. It took her only three strides to reach him. She placed her hand between his legs.

He chuckled. "Honey, you got to give me time to recharge. Come on put on one of your sexy dresses and come with me."

She let go of him, put her hands on her hips and struck a model's pose, one leg slightly behind the other, her face turned at an angle with pouty lips. "I don't feel like getting dressed up."

He stepped into his leopard-print briefs. "That's okay. You can put on those designer jeans and your Armani sweatshirt. Be nice and comfortable. When we get to the club I'll buy you some Jamaican ganja and we'll mellow out."

"Fuck it. You want to go so bad, go by yourself. I'll stay here, order out and smoke a joint while I wait for the food." She sashayed back to bed.

"Oh, please, baby, come with me." He clasped his hands in front of his chest, begging for her cooperation.

"I told you I'm staying here." She slid down and pulled the sheet over her head.

I'm fucked, DeMarcus thought. He crept to the bed, sat on the edge and lifted the sheet off of Marti's face. "Baby, I's going to surprise you but you forcing me to tell you my plans for the night. I have my boss lady and her man meeting us there. 'Cause as of tonight I's out of the game and asking to you to marry me."

She gave him a stunned look, then jumped up and wrapped her arms around his neck, "Oh my God, DeMarcus. I love you. I want to go with you wherever you want."

"Then come with me to listen to some reggae."

"I'd love to."

Chapter 43

9:30 PM

Luka drove the van and Sergei and Mikhail their cars up and down the Near North neighborhood, but found no trace of Scott Garity. "This son of bitch must be shacking up with some broad," Drazen told them over his cell when they reported in. "Luka and me will go back to his house and wait there. Sergei, you and Mikhail stay up here and look for him. We find him, we find Marti. Then we take care of business."

Scott rested his hands on Ashley's slender waist and looked into her eyes. "I need your help tonight."

"I think I already did that."

"You did, but I need you even more."

She smiled. "How's that?"

"I don't think the guy that was supposed to meet me can make it. The FBI is on him."

"What *is* this with the FBI? They're on your buddy and you think they followed you. Is this some major crime you're getting me involved in?"

"I told you what it's about. They want to use Marti to get the Russian and the Governor. Once they use her, they'll deport her because if she was smuggled into the country you can bet she's not here legally. She goes back to Europe, where who knows what will happen to her. The Russian will call the same idiots that kidnapped her. She'll be dead before she's nineteen."

"Okay, Sir Lancelot."

"There's more."

"You're kidding. What?"

"She's going to need a place to stay until—"

She shook her head and her hair fell over her face. "No way, I'm not keeping her here. This is my home. It's my sanctuary away from all the shit that goes on in this world."

With one finger, Scott tucked her hair behind her ear. "Ashley, Marti is you twenty years ago."

"Bullshit. Even so, I survived. She can, too."

"It'll only be for a while. You do this one thing for me, I'll be forever indebted to you."

Her eyes widened. "How long is a while'?"

"I don't know exactly."

"Why can't she stay with you?"

"The FBI has been at my house. They don't know about you and I've got my kid. I don't want Billy seeing them busting into my house. The G's probably sitting on my car now." Scott paused and his voice softened. "Can you call us a cab?"

Fifteen minutes later they raced down the stairs of Ashley's greystone and hopped into a Yellow cab. They head north on Dearborn Parkway as Sergei drove past them in his Audi heading south.

Chapter 44

Reggae Club

Scott and Ashley left the cab and entered the club. The aroma of ganja hit him. "I hope you don't have to take a drug test," he said.

"Wouldn't matter, I probably wouldn't pass it anyway." Ashley laughed. "We should have stopped at a head shop and bought you a baseball cap with the corn roll wig. It'd help you fit in. Could be a good look for you, too."

"You're always looking out for my best interests."

"I'm here, right?"

"You got me there." He gazed across the dimly lit room. To their right were a series of bar tables pushed against the wall and standing room only for the customers hovering around them. To the right, the bar was equally crowded. The customers gazed at the band as they drained their drinks and gyrated to the music. Smoke from their joints and cigarettes curled to the ceiling.

Straight ahead was the stage, barely large enough for the four-man band. The lead singer, barefoot, wore a red tank top with a picture of Bob

Marley, black and green board shorts, and had stuffed his corn rolls into a red and green Rasta hat. He waved his arms and his head bobbed up and down to the beat as he sang. On the keyboard was an out-of-place white dude, and more Rasta men on the drums and rhythm guitar.

"You see them?" Scott asked.

"No, but they'll be here." She nodded toward a table. "That couple is leaving. Let's grab it." Ashley rushed to the table, laying claim to it. Scott followed.

A black waitress dressed in a long tank top with black, green and yellow stripes that flashed her chocolate cleavage and stopped at midthigh strolled up to the table. "Good evening. We have two for one specials tonight on Red Stripe and piña coladas."

"I'll have the piña coladas, "Ashley said.

"I'll have a Coke." Scott glanced at his watch. It was ten-fifteen.

"No problem, man." The waitress went to the bar to get their drinks.

"You're the life of the party," Ashley said.

Scott tapped his right hip.

She grasped the meaning of his gesture. "Oh."

The waitress returned with their drinks. Scott's was a frosted glass of Coca-Cola, Ashley's two glasses with orange paper umbrellas and slices of pineapple.

"When did you talk to him last?" Meaning DeMarcus DeWayne.

She pulled an umbrella out of her first drink, ate the slice of pineapple and chugged half of the drink as Scott waited for an answer. She put the glass back on the table, picked up a napkin and dabbed her lips. "Hm, that's good. I'm glad I'm not strapped. I called him last night. Don't worry about it."

Scott sighed. "You should have checked with him today."

"I promise you he'll be here."

"With Marti?"

"Definitely. You know women. She's probably taking some time to dress and they might be looking for a parking spot. In this neighborhood that could take a while."

Scott leaned against the wall and perused the crowd, looking for anyone that might be an FBI agent or a Russian. Everyone he saw looked like patrons of the bar. When the band took a break, he glanced at his watch. "It's ten-thirty. Maybe you should call DeMarcus?"

"Give him another fifteen minutes and if they don't show, I'll call."

Scott exhaled and took a sip of his Coke. He pulled out his cell phone. "Give me his number. I'll call him."

Ashley dug her phone out of her purse. Before she could check the address book, a black hand grasped hers.

"You looking for me?" DeMarcus said.

"You're late. Remember what I told you about being late?" Ashley said.

Scott felt DeMarcus' gaze drift to him. "You the guy that slapped my El Do the other night. Scared the shit out of me."

Scott looked the pimp in the eyes. "Where's Marti?"

"I dropped her off at the front door and went lookin' for a parking space. She should be here."

"Son of a bitch." Scott looked at Ashley. "I told you to call him. We could have met her at the door. Now—" He shook his head. "Who knows what happened to her."

"What's all the commotion about?" Marti came up to the table and put her arm around DeMarcus' shoulders. She wore painted-on jeans, a white cardigan with the top four buttons undone and red high heels. "Did you tell them, honey?"

DeMarcus glanced at the floor. Ashley grabbed her second drink and took a long slug.

"We're getting married." Marti kissed DeMarcus on his cheek.

Ashley yanked the glass from her mouth, slamming it on the table. She covered her lips with one hand, snorting and laughing at the same time.

Marti propped her hands on her hips. "What's so funny?" She glanced at DeMarcus, who looked away from her. "You dick, was this just a line of bullshit to get me here?"

DeMarcus grabbed her hand. "I love you, baby. But I don't deserve you." He shook his head. "I'd make you a terrible husband."

"He's not lying to you now." Ashley laughed and took another gulp of her drink.

Marti shook his hand away and turned toward the door.

Scott grabbed her arm and pulled her back to the table. "You want to get clean and not have to worry about the Russian."

She stared at him. "Who're you?"

"I know your story, I know the people that want to hurt you, and I can help you get what you want."

DeMarcus took her other hand. "See, baby, I do love you and that's why I brung you here tonight. 'Cause I knew this man was going to help you."

She dropped his hand. Her gaze shifted from DeMarcus back to Scott. "So who're you, why do you want to help me, and why should I believe you?"

Ashley waved her hand. "DeMarcus works for me. I told him to bring you here tonight so Scott," she nodded at him, "so Scott could meet you. He was a federal agent. He's as straight as they come."

Marti still looked wary. "So now I know who he is, but not why he would help me. How do I know he's not working for Drazen?"

"Marti, I know you haven't any reason to trust me," Scott said. "But DeMarcus brought you here and he's protected you so far. I know four things. You took money from the Russian. He wants it back. You don't have the money and you want to get clean. I can help you with all of those things. This is the only chance you'll get to resolve all these issues."

"Resolving issues, there you go talking like a shrink again," Ashley said.

Scott gave her a sidelong glance.

Marti tilted her head. "So how do you know so much?"

Scott gave her a level stare. "You'll have to trust me. Or you can keep turning tricks, stashing your cash and maybe by the time you're thirty you'll have enough to go to rehab—that is, if the dope doesn't kill you before the Russian does. You know he has to make an example out of you. He doesn't want his other girls running away."

She swallowed. "So what do I have to do?"

"You, Ashley and me are going to take a cab to Ashley's place. You're going to stay with her for a few days until my plan is finished.

Chapter 45

They all got out of the cab and marched up the stairs to Ashley's house. Scott looked over his shoulder for anyone following them. He saw no one. They entered and he locked the door, then rushed to the living room and peered through the break in the curtains. No one appeared to be watching the building, no car idling in front of it. He thought, *too easy, too easy.*

Marti stood in the foyer, mesmerized by the elegantly designed interior. "This is all yours?"

Ashley pointed to the white leather sofa. "Sit down, you might as well make yourself at home since you're going to be staying for a few days." She turned, looked at Scott standing at the curtain, and headed to the bar. "How long is your plan going to take?"

Scott walked over to the bar and shrugged.

Ashley poured herself an amaretto over ice. "The usual for you, Scott?"

He nodded and his cell phone rang. The display reflected Father Dugan's number. He pushed the talk button. "How was the movie?"

The answering voice was a stranger's, with a slight Russian accent. "Your priest doesn't feel like talking right now."

A chill went through him. "Who's this?"

"I'm a friend of Marti's. How is she?"

Scott marched out of the living room into the foyer. "What do you want?"

"Garity, you know what I want. You bring her to me now."

Scott paused. "I don't have her. Don't know where she is."

"You're lying to me. I have it from a good source that you expected to get her tonight."

Everson, Scott thought. "You should get a better source. How did you get this phone?"

"The priest gave it to me. He's much more cooperative than you are. But then, he doesn't want to see your boy hurt."

His gut tightened. "Where's Billy?"

"You don't understand. As you Americans say, I'm holding all the cards. I'll ask the questions and you'll do what I say."

"Put my son on the phone. That's the only way I know you have him."

"Come, come, Garity. That's not the only way. If you don't think I have Billy, I can send you one of his fingers or maybe his ear. I'm sure that will convince you."

Scott fought to keep his voice level. "Put Father Dugan on the phone."

"He doesn't feel like talking right now. I make you a deal. You have twenty-four hours to bring me the girl. Call me on this phone. It's up to you. You don't call, I take one of your boy's fingers. One each day until you bring her."

"You son of a bitch, you hurt my boy and I'll kill—"

The line went dead. Scott let his arms drop to his sides, took a deep breath and stared at the floor. *My plan. What is it now?*

Ashley tapped his shoulder and whispered, "How long do you think Marti will be here?"

Before he could answer, Marti followed close behind with a question of her own. "What is your plan for me, sir?"

Scott exhaled. *I wish I knew.*

Chapter 46

Scott met Marti's eyes. He could see she was waiting to find out what was going to happen to her.

"Sir?" she said. Her brow furrowed with anxiety and her eyes welled. She looked at him as if her whole world depended on what he said in the next few minutes.

He put his hand on her shoulder, trying to give her some sense of security. "I have to call some people and then you'll be set. Ashley, can you take Marti upstairs and run a warm bath for her while I make a few calls?"

Ashley nodded. He watched her take Marti's hand, and the two of them walked up the stairs and disappeared into her master bedroom suite.

Scott hit Haller's number on his cell.

Haller answered within two rings. "Scott? What's going on?"

"FBI with you?"

"No, I'm home. They might be parked outside, but they're not with me now."

"I've got a big problem. I'm at Ashley's with Marti. The Russian called on Father Dugan's cell. He said he's got Billy. He wouldn't let me talk to my boy or Father Dugan. Said he wants Marti in twenty-four hours, or he'll cut one of Billy's fingers off for each day he doesn't have her."

"Fuck, you can't risk it. You've got to get the FBI involved."

He felt a nerve in his neck twitch, and his head throbbed. "I wanted this to be nice and clean and it's really fucked up now. I can't think straight. I'll give Richmond a call. I told him I'd call him if this lead worked out. I'll be in touch." He ended the phone call, thinking that right now he'd do almost anything for a handful of Vicodin.

He went to the voicemails on his phone and hit the message Richmond had left. The phone rang six times, and then he heard Richmond's voicemail greeting. The phone beeped, waiting to record a message. Scott cancelled the call.

He looked at his watch. Twelve-fifteen. He had been clean for four days. Right now, though, he craved something to dull the stress he was feeling. Without realizing it, he started scratching the back of his left hand, each scratch digging deeper and deeper. His gaze flashed toward the bar. He rushed over, bashing his foot on the leg of the coffee table and almost tripping en route. He swore as he leaned into the bar, poured a jigger of Scotch into a glass and downed it. *This will have to do.* He filled the glass again, walked to the curtains and peered out the window. *God help me if anything happens to Billy.* Blood dripped from his scratched hand onto the hardwood floor.

His phone rang. The display read *unknown*. He let the phone ring until it went to voicemail. "Scott, it's Richmond. I saw you called me. Don't be stupid. If something's on, you'll need my help. If you don't call you, could be in big trouble." The line went dead.

Scott held the phone and just stared at it. He had to figure out what to do, but his brain felt like frozen slush.

A little time passed. Ashley and Marti both went to bed. Scott lay down on the sofa. He couldn't sleep. He took the bottle of Scotch from the bar and set it on the coffee table. Stupid, *stupid*, to have put his son in jeopardy. A few drinks and two hours later, his phone rang. Caller ID *unknown*. Scott let it go to voicemail.

"Garity, it's Richmond. If you don't call me and something goes down, I promise you at a minimum I'll get a warrant for you for obstruction of justice. I can't make it any simpler than that. Call me."

Scott went to the list of calls received and saw two entries: Richmond's *unknown* and Father Dugan's number. He hit the one he knew he had to.

Chapter 47

"You've got the girl?" Drazen Ivanov asked.

"Yes," Scott said.

"I don't like this. I talk to you a couple of hours ago and you tell me you don't have her. Now all of sudden you do. I should cut off a finger for you lying to me."

"It wasn't a lie. I didn't have her then. I knew where she was supposed to be and I found her there."

"Yeah, yeah, yeah. You lie to me again and I cut off your boy's hand. Can you live with yourself knowing you crippled your boy?"

"I'm not lying. Is he okay?"

"He's a good boy."

"And Father Dugan?"

"I'm a generous man. I give you two for one. You will find me a man of my word, not like you. You and the girl come and no one else. You bring cops or friends, you get your boy and the priest in pieces. You hear me?"

Scott swallowed. "I hear you."

Ivanov laughed. "Good. Then this be over soon and everyone happy. You bring the girl to me at four. That gives you just about an hour." He gave Scott an address. "You know where this is?"

He did, or thought so, and his heart sank. "I can find it."

"You park by the wood fence in the parking lot behind the building. I have people watching, so don't be stupid. In pieces, remember?"

The call ended abruptly. Scott saw Marti coming down the stairs wearing a white terry cloth robe.

"Was that Drazen?" she asked.

Scott nodded.

"I'm causing you so much trouble. What did he say?"

"He's holding my son and our priest to trade for you."

"You know he will kill me for stealing that money. And if you don't bring me to him, he will kill your son and the priest." She hid her face in her hands.

"Don't worry I'll figure something out. I have to make another call." He punched in Haller's number as he watched Marti walk into the living room and collapse onto the couch. "Joe, I know what you said. But I don't trust the FBI. They'll use Marti to make a case and then deport her. I just talked with the Russian. I'm going to meet him at the apartment building you found. At four, about an hour from now. Can you make it?"

"You're a shithead."

"I really need you, Joe."

"You're a shithead and I'm a dummy. I'll be there."

"Thanks, Joe. I'm supposed to park in the lot behind and call him. Try to find a space where you can eyeball us, but don't get burned. I want my kid in one piece."

"No pressure. Just one question."

"What's that?"

He laughed. "How're you ever going to repay me?"

Chapter 48

3:45 AM

SCOTT PULLED HIS OLDSMOBILE CUTLASS into the crowded parking lot behind Ivanov's building. A row of cars was parked next to the rear of the building and another row against an old wooden fence that leaned toward the lot. The fence was missing several slats. The wind gusted and light from the lamppost danced across Scott's face. He double-parked in front of the cars parked against the fence. Marti slid down in the passenger seat.

Scott looked up at the third floor apartment. Light shone through the barred windows. He took his cell out of his shirt pocket and called Father Dugan's number. The phone rang five times. Above, the lights went out. Then came a tap on his window, steel hitting glass. Scott looked over and saw a large man with a .45 semi-auto pointed at the back of his head.

"Open door," the gunman said in broken English.

Scott twisted to his left and pulled the lock button up on the rear door. The huge man slid in behind him. Scott felt the pistol barrel jab him behind his left ear. A meaty arm came over Scott's right shoulder. One plate-sized hand slid around Scott's waistband until it found his Sig Sauer. The gunman yanked it out and stuck it in his own pants. "You have anything else, tell me now or you be sorry."

"No, that's it."

The man fell back against the rear seat with a thud. "Hello, Marti."

She answered in a small voice. "Hello, Luka."

"Garity, you do what I tell you. I take you to your boy. Pull onto street and go west."

Scott tugged on the steering wheel and followed Luka's instructions. As he turned, he saw Haller's Chevrolet parked on the opposite side of the street.

"Where're we going?" Scott asked.

Luka jabbed his pistol harder against the back of Scott's neck. "Shut up. Just go where I tell you." Luka's phone rang, and he pulled it out of his shirt pocket. "I have them." A pause as he turned and looked out the back window. "Mikhail and Sergei behind us. Don't see anyone else. Okay, Papa." He shut the phone off and stuffed it back in his pocket, then nudged Marti's shoulder with the barrel of his pistol. "Drazen say to tell you don't be scared."

Marti's chin sank to her chest. A tear rolled down her cheek.

Scott followed Luka's directions and went north on Mannheim Road past O'Hare Airport. Ten minutes later he headed northwest on Route 14. A few miles after that, Luka ordered him to park in back of a shopping center off the highway.

"Shut car off. We get out here." Luka waved his pistol.

Scott got out of the car. Letters painted on the back of a steel door across the way read *Petersburg Real Estate Corporation*. The shopping center Ivanov owned, that Haller had told him about.

Luka banged on the steel door with his fist. Two deadbolts clicked and the hinges squealed as the door opened toward them. Luka pushed them inside, into a dark room. The door slammed behind them and the deadbolts clicked again. Scott heard the snap of a chain, and the flash of a light bulb cast his shadow across the cement floor. To his right were seven wooden skids with banker's storage boxes piled three feet high. To the left he saw a 21-inch TV on a black stand, below it a CD player and in front two wooden chairs with arms. Tied to the chairs and gagged were Father Dugan and Billy.

Billy twisted in his chair. Scott rushed to him and pulled off the gag. "Are you okay?"

"Yeah." Billy sounded scared but tried not to show it. "Why did they take me?"

Scott didn't answer. He scrabbled at the rope around Billy's arms. From the corner of his eye he saw motion, too late to avoid Luka as the big man stepped forward, grabbed Scott by his hair and tossed him to the floor.

Scott fell onto his back. He ignored the jolt of pain, propped himself up with his hands and looked at Drazen Ivanov. "I brought you the girl. You said you were a man of your word. Now you can prove it. Let me take my son and the priest and leave."

"I wish I could. But things have changed." Drazen pointed at Marti. "If for some reason this bitch disappears, there are now three witnesses that last saw her here. That's not so good for me."

The steel door opened and two more men entered. Mikhail and Sergei, Scott guessed. They closed the door and leaned against the wall.

"But she's alive and well. That's all we could say," Scott said.

"I don't think I can trust you to say that to the authorities."

"I work for the governor," Scott said, desperate. "He calls me his man. What kind of man works for him? A man who understands that sometimes things have to be sacrificed for the benefit of those in power."

Drazen laughed. "Garity, you sound like a Greek philosopher. So intelligent, and so stupid to think I would fall for your bullshit. If this whore had never stolen the governor's money, none of us would be here now. As it is, I have to avenge my son's death. Luka took care of the nigger dope dealer that killed Marko. Now I deal with the whore." He nodded at one of the thugs near the door. "Sergei, put a CD in the player. Dance for us, Marti. She's really quite good."

Sergai grabbed a disk on top of the CD player. "D. Throne," he said. "Heavy metal." He looked at Drazen, who nodded. Sergei grinned as the other thug—Mikhail—grabbed Marti by the arm and spun her to the center of the room. "Dance like you used to do for us," Sergei said.

Loud and angry-sounding, the music banged against the walls. Marti glanced at Scott, her face a blank mask of terror, as she started to sway her hips.

"Take that sweater off," Mikhail said. "I want to see the dragon."

She undid the top three buttons, revealing the valley between her breasts.

Scott stepped in front of Billy, blocking his view. He remembered the newspaper article Richmond had shown him. "You're mistaken, Drazen. About that dope dealer. The only person killed where your son died was a sixteen-year old girl visiting her grandmother."

Drazen sneered. "You think you're so clever, Garity. Luka killed the nigger that killed Marko. Mikhail and Sergei were there and saw him."

"That's right, I shot the nigger. He died on the stairs right where he murdered Marko." Luka's gaze shot toward Mikhail and then Sergei, as if awaiting their confirmation.

Scott pointed at Luka. "You coward. First you shoot a teenage girl, then you lie to the man you call Papa so you can fool him into thinking you're as good as his son was."

Luka pulled a pistol out of his pants, raised it to shoulder height and pointed it at Scott. "You want to die in front of your son?"

"That would be like you. Kill me in front of Billy, and then I suppose you'll shoot him and Father Dugan. You're the best qualified. You've already killed a child."

"You son of bitch." Luka pulled back the hammer on the semi-auto.

"Mikhail, Sergei, tell us. Who did Luka shoot?" Scott said.

Drazen smirked. "Tell him."

Mikhail dragged his arm across his forehead, wiping off beads of perspiration.

Drazen frowned. "Tell him."

Mikhail pursed his lips and looked at Sergei.

Drazen's gaze shifted to Sergei. "Who did Luka shoot?"

Sergei eyed Drazen, then Luka. "He shot someone on the stairs. We didn't stop to see who it was. We ran up to the apartment and shot the door down."

"And the dope dealer was in the apartment?" Drazen asked.

"No one was in the apartment," Mikhail said. "The next day the newspaper said a young girl was killed by gangs."

Drazen shifted his weight and glanced at the floor. Then he raised his head and focused on Luka. "I call you my son. I ask you to avenge my real son's death. A noble deed. A deed that should have brought joy. Because the man that killed my son was not worthy of living." Drazen shook his head. "You tell me that I will never have to question your loyalty. That you want revenge just like I did."

Sergei stepped forward. "He told us we must never speak of our failure to kill the people at the drug house. Not even to you."

Drazen was still staring at Luka. "And you said you were happy you could do this for me." He yanked a Makarov PM semi-auto pistol from under his coat."

Luka turned from Scott to Drazen. "No, Papa. No."

Shots exploded through the room. Scott dived toward Billy, knocking the chair and him over. He heard glass shattering and something huge come crashing through the drywall in the front of the room. A car, he saw as it skidded to stop two feet from him.

Joe Haller jumped out of the car, pistol in hand, and ran to Scott.

"Untie Father Dugan. I'll get Billy," Scott said. "Take the priest and back out if your car is still working. I'll take Billy and Marti in my car. "

Sergei and Mikhail ran outside through the broken wall. Scott paid them little attention. He untied Billy and then looked around for Marti. She was on her knees, holding Drazen's head. He grabbed Billy's hand

and ran to her. A bloody hole gaped where Drazen's right eye had been. Blood leaked onto Marti's jeans where the back of his skull had been blown away. Scott glanced ten feet to his right at Luka, prone on the floor, blood spurting from a wound in his throat. "We've got to get out of here before the cops come."

Marti stroked Drazen's forehead. "He always treated me well. It was my fault. I stole the money."

With his free hand Scott grabbed her and brought her to her feet. They ran to the rear door. Scott turned the deadbolts, and the three of them fled the building and jumped into his car. Then he remembered. *My fucking pistol.*

He flung himself out of the car and ran back inside the building. The smell of cordite hung in the air. Luka's corpse held his Sig Sauer. *Fuck.* He pried Luka's fingers open, grabbed his pistol and took a precious few seconds to locate the ejected shell casing on the floor. *Who knows where the bullet went. Can't look for it now.*

He took Luka's .45 out of the man's waistband and fired a round into the ceiling. Then he wiped the grips with his coat sleeve, placed it in Luka's hand and wrapped the man's fingers around them. *Hope the cops don't find the bullet from my Sig.*

He ran back out to his Cutlass. The tires squealed against the pavement as the shriek of distant sirens grew louder.

Chapter 49

5:00 AM

Scott drove to St. Mary's. Haller's Chevy was parked in front of the rectory. The bumper hung six inches lower on the driver's side and there was a crease across the width of the hood. He parked behind the Chevy, woke Billy who'd fallen asleep in the rear seat of the Cutlass, and took him and Marti into the building.

Light shone into the darkened hallway from the open door to Father Dugan's office. When they entered, Scott saw Dugan sitting behind his desk and Haller in an armchair in front of it.

Marti dragged herself to a worn cloth couch against the opposite wall. Her jeans were soaked with the Russian's blood. Billy lay down on the other side of the sofa and laid his head on the armrest.

"Father, I'm sorry, it's my fault," Scott said. "I thought the FBI followed me here when I dropped Billy off. Obviously it was the Russians. Are you all right?"

The priest's hair was plastered across his head as if he had just woken from a bad night's sleep. He opened a side drawer, lifted out a bottle of Jameson's and three glasses, and placed them on his desk. He screwed off the cap and poured a few ounces in each glass. He picked one up, brought it to his lips, and drained it. "I will be now." He waved his hands over the remaining glasses.

Haller reached for one with a trembling hand and took a sip.

Scott sat in a chair next to Haller. "You came in the nick of time."

Haller emptied his glass and set it on the desk. "I went to the front door. It was locked. Got back to my car when I heard the shots. The only thing I could do was drive through the plate glass window and the drywall. Got to figure out what to tell the insurance company."

Scott looked over his shoulder. Marti sat with her head propped against the wall, mouth open and eyes closed. Billy was curled up on the sofa. Both were fast asleep. Scott leaned forward, resting his forearms on his thighs. "I went back in after I realized the big guy, Luka, still had my Sig. I found it in his hand. He grabbed my gun out of his waistband instead of his .45." Scott took a deep breath and exhaled. "He shot the Russian with my pistol. I found the shell casing. Didn't have time to look for the bullet. Hopefully, the cops won't find it."

The priest held the bottle over Haller's glass.

"No thanks, Father." He held up his hand. It was steady. "I just broke about four years of sobriety. I don't want to overdo it. One was all I needed to settle down."

"Sorry, my lad. I didn't know you were an AA member. Scotty?"

"No." He nodded at Haller. "He's my sponsor. I had a few earlier and I feel like it'll be coming back up soon."

Haller looked at Scott. "So where do we go from here?"

"In about five hours we'll be at the Governor's law office. Whether he wants us or not."

CHAPTER 50

Everson's Law Office

SCOTT AND MARTI ENTERED THE lobby. He wore his usual tan corduroy sport coat and jeans. Marti had on black slacks and a white pullover they'd purchased at Wal-Mart an hour ago. He looked at Jeanie on the other side of the glass partition. She frowned—either wary or puzzled, Scott wasn't sure. Maybe both.

"Is he in?" Scott asked.

She picked up the phone. "I'll let him know you're here."

He reached through the opening and put his hand on the receiver. "Come with us. We'll surprise him."

She buzzed the door. Scott held it open and Marti walked through it. Jeanie stood up at her desk. "What's this about?"

"Let's say, security for everyone." Scott led the way down the hall, stopped at the closed door to Everson's office, grabbed the doorknob and turned it.

Two men, well-dressed and clearly associates of Everson's, occupied the chairs in front of the desk. They, and Everson, looked startled to see him. "Scott, we're in the middle of a meeting right now. I'm booked for the day," Everson said. "Check with Jeanie to see when she can fit you in."

"I've got someone I want you to meet." Scott grabbed Marti by the arm and pulled her through the doorway.

The governor pushed back his chair. "This, ah…this is an important meeting. Why don't you come back tonight? Say after seven, and then—"

"Come on, Governor. I'm your man. I thought you'd always have time for me. And you told me how important it was that I find Marti. Well, here she is."

Everson glanced at the two suits sitting in front of him. "Go work on the motions we've discussed. I'll get back with you as soon as this matter is resolved."

"James, we need to file this with the court before the judge breaks for lunch," one of the suits said.

Everson flicked his right hand, "Jesus Christ, Lerman, I said I'll get back to you. Now finalize the fucking motions." He grabbed the papers on his desk and spun them at Lerman.

Clearly irritated, Lerman grabbed the stack with both hands and marched out of the office. His colleague followed.

Everson waved Scott, Marti and Jeanie inside. "Close the goddamn door. Scott, this better be good."

"Oh, it is, Gov. Maybe the best thing that ever happened to you." Scott sat in a vacated chair. "Marti, you sit here next to me." he tapped the arm of the second chair. "Jeanie, pull up that chair from against the wall and sit on this side of me."

He waited a moment while both women got settled, then continued speaking. "Governor, let me make a formal introduction. This is Marti, the young lady, as you told me, daughter of one of your European clients, whom you reported to me as missing. As you can see, she's in good health and one piece."

Everson scowled. "Get on with it. What is it that you want?"

Scott lounged in his chair. "It's come to my attention that certain funds in a bank account have recently become Jeanie's responsibility—"

The governor shook his head spittle flying off his lips. "Don't think you're going to steal my money. You son of a bitch."

Scott shook his head. "Governor, this is all about legacy. We know your untarnished reputation as a former governor of Illinois is important to you and your party. What I'm about to propose will only enhance your reputation." He stood, walked around Everson's desk, sat on the corner and rested one foot on the armrest of Everson's chair.

The ex-governor leaned away from Scott, eyes narrowed and lips pursed.

Scott leaned forward until their faces were inches apart. "First, your law firm will represent Marti and all the girls smuggled in by Drazen Ivanov so they can gain their citizenship. Second, the funds in the accounts managed by Jeanie—the ones Marchese use to handle for you—will be deposited into a new account. Also deposited into this account will be the balance of your campaign funds. This new account will be used to fund the James Everson Foundation. One more star to put on your tombstone. The purpose of this foundation will be treatment, rehabilitation and recovery for drug addicts and victims of white slavery. The first group of patients will be Marti, her dancer friends and anyone else the governor's man feels would be appropriate. This foundation will be managed by Jeanie and her pay will be increased by twenty thousand." Scott straightened, letting his words sink in.

Everson's face had gone ashen. "Really, and what if I—"

"Thanks to you, I have some new acquaintances in the FBI. Fight me on this and we'll be leaving here so Marti and Jeanie can give their statements to special agents Richmond and O'Malley.

He slid off the desk and stood upright. "Let me know your preference, because otherwise we're on our way."

Epilogue

FORMER GOVERNOR JAMES EVERSON SAW fit to generously donate his campaign funds and monies from other sources to the newly formed Everson Foundation. The dancers from the Pole Club obtained their citizenship based on political asylum and successfully completed their rehabilitation. One other patient did likewise. But he was never again referred to as the governor's man.